When one seeks to pursue virtue to extremes, vices emerge.

—Pascal

Every day confirms my opinion on the superiority of a vicious life—and if Virtue is not its own reward, I don't know any other stipend that can be attached to it.

—Lord Byron

Every virtue has its indecent literature.

—Louis Ferdinand Céline

Other BOOKS and PARODIES
by TONY HENDRA

The 80s: A Look Back (Edited with Christopher
  Cerf and Peter Elbling)
The 90s: A Look Back (Edited with Peter Elbling)

Not The New York Times (Edited with
  Christopher Cerf and George Plimpton)
Off the Wall Street Journal I & II (Editor-in-Chief)
Meet Mr. Bomb (Editor-in-Chief)

THE SAYINGS OF AYATOLLAH KHOMEINI
NOT THE BIBLE (with Sean Kelly)
GOING TOO FAR
TALES FROM THE CRIB (with Bob Saget)
BORN TO RUN THINGS: An Utterly Unauthorized
  Biography of George Bush
BRAD 61 (Based on the paintings of Roy
  Lichtenstein)

The Book
of
Bad Virtues

A TREASURY
OF IMMORALITY

A Parody by

TONY HENDRA

POCKET BOOKS

New York   London   Toronto   Sydney   Tokyo   Singapore

To Nicholas, Sebastian, and Lucy Hendra
And to P.M. —who made me do it.

THE BOOK OF CREATION and CHRIST—THE EARLY YEARS were originally published in NOT THE BIBLE, Ballantine Books, copyright 1983 by Tony Hendra and Sean Kelly.

DETERIORATA copyright 1971 Tony Hendra first appeared in the *National Lampoon*.

THE HAMILTON PHILADELPHIA LETTER first appeared in the *199th Birthday Book* copyright 1975 *National Lampoon*. Used by permission.

SHIT HAPPENS suggested by George Carlin.

An *Original* Publication of POCKET BOOKS

POCKET BOOKS, a division of Simon & Schuster Inc.
1230 Avenue of the Americas, New York, NY 10020

ISBN: 0-671-51928-X

First Pocket Books trade paperback printing December 1994

10 9 8 7 6 5 4 3 2 1

POCKET and colophon are registered trademarks of Simon & Schuster Inc.

Text design by Stanley S. Drate/Folio Graphics Co., Inc.

Printed in the U.S.A.

CONTENTS

· III ·
GREED

55

· IV ·
SLACKING

73

· V ·
SELF-INDULGENCE

99

· VI ·
EGOTISM 121

· VII ·
BLASPHEMY 141

· VIII ·
COLD HARD-HEARTEDNESS 159

· IX ·
SEXING AND DRUGGING   183

INTRODUCTION

Things are a mess. Johnny can't read. Johnny wears his baseball cap backwards. Johnny has a sawed-off shotgun in his gym bag. Jane can't read either, and in her gym bag there's a diaphragm. What's a worried parent to do? Easy. Shackle Johnny and Jane to their beds and instill family values in them. Read them a folk tale from a simpler age when families stuck together and respected each other. Because if they didn't: a) there'd be no harvest and they'd starve, and b) the nobles who owned them and the land they lived on would beat them to a bloody pulp.

Folk tales should give Johnny pause the next time he feels like breaking into the Defense Department's classified files. Folk tales'll give Jane second thoughts as she contemplates going all the way with a Vietnamese-Samoan hunk called Rodriguez in the back of a 1977 Trans Am. Yes siree Bob. Traditional values are what Jane and Johnny need.

The traditional American virtues being touted in the 1990s are overwhelmingly those of nineteenth-century England, exemplified by the prose and poetry that Victorians deemed improving. As our social conditions more closely parallel those of the 1890s—a vast disparity between rich and poor, Dickensian conditions in the slums, tidal waves of immigration, crises in public health, resurgent racial conflict, bulging prisons, rapid growth of mysterious new technologies, trouble in the Balkans, etc.—neo-Victorianism makes sense. Trouble is, the Victorian virtues we look back on so wistfully weren't the rock-solid values of a happy and stable society; on the contrary, they were a desperate attempt to impose some order on the social chaos wrought by the Industrial Revolution. To counter it, Victorians looked back to earlier, simpler times for inspiration, in particular to the Middle Ages—which is why Victorian fairy stories and children's books were medieval in style and illustration. For their part, the medievals, beset by the social upheaval of mercantilism and under constant threat from the world of Islam, looked back to the early Church for spiritual purity and to Rome for civic virtues. The Roman Empire, in turmoil throughout its history, looked back to earlier times for calmer certainties. As did the Greeks. The late Egyptians looked back fondly on the Middle Egyptians in whose eyes the early Egyptians found favor. The Babylonians doubtless thought the Sumerians had been simpler, more decent folk than themselves. And so on.

The urge to invoke the past for values and virtues echoes back down the millennia to the very dawn of civilization around 8000 B.C., when hunter–gatherers first organized themselves into grain-growing communities. It would be reassuring to think that they came together to establish embryonic family values and civic virtues. No such luck. According to prominent anthropologists like Solomon Katz and Mary Voigt, they did so to ferment the grain and ensure themselves a steady supply of beer. Humanity's first (and possibly finest) impulse, far from instilling discipline, responsibility, honesty, obedience, and other moral virtues into Johnny and Jane, seems to have been to leave them to their own devices and get drunk. (There is, of course, the alternative explanation that moral virtues were invented to keep Johnny and Jane busy while humanity popped down to the brewing shed to see how the latest batch was coming.)

If there never was an Eden of family values and civic virtue, what lies behind the conservative desire to reach back to it? Probably that they confuse a historic earlier, simpler time with their own personal earlier, simpler time—to wit, that brief Eden of certitude between the ages of four and seven, when consciousness has emerged, every experience is for the first time, and parents are still large and loved. Pat Buchanan, for example, doesn't want to remake America so much as return to the America of Westbrook Pegler and the Brooklyn Dodgers, when drugs came from the drugstore and Mass was in Latin. In short, when he was six—and safe. Pat (not to mention Rush and the other Pat) must warm to the words of that splendidly Victorian sentimentalist A. A. Milne:

> When I was three, I was hardly me
> When I was four, I was not much more
> When I was five, I was just alive
> But now I am six, I'm as clever as clever
> I think I'll be six now for ever and ever.

This isn't to let liberals off the hook. If your conservative is an eternal six-year-old, your liberal is an eternal sixteen-year-old, forever rebellious, forever oblivious to the nasty realities of life, forever looking *forward* to some impossible revolution in human nature. It's when either of these dolts gets to run public policy that they become truly ridiculous. What's even more absurd than a loudmouthed sexagenarian six-year-old? A deeply concerned sexagenarian teenager. It's time for everyone to get in touch with his or her inner grown-up.

Of course, every age needs its official virtues, millennial Americans no less than medieval clerics or Ming Dynasty mandarins. Only a moron would imagine, however, that because people once put these codes of conduct in writing they lived up to them. Ought is one thing, Is is another.

The two are not supposed to mix. People who insist on living official virtues to the letter usually cause, or get into, huge amounts of trouble. Look at Jesus. Look at Jimmy Carter. Hypocrisy is what keeps society humming. Public pieties are to be intoned at the appropriate moments, such as elections or executions; the rest of the time people get on with the business of skimming, boasting, goofing off, ducking responsibility, lusting, eating, beating the odds, and popping down to the brewing shed to see how the latest batch is coming.

These activities used to be called Vices, but Don Johnson and Philip Michael Thomas gave Vice a bad name. Henceforth Vices shall be known as Bad Virtues. There ought to be seven of them just as there used to be seven Vices; however, we live in the Age of Top Ten. We'll settle for nine on the principle that there are nine circles in Hell, and Dante Alighieri knew more about the subject than Dave does.

This book celebrates the Nine Bad Virtues. It won't teach Johnny and Jane how to practice them. (If they're normal kids, they know already.) In fact it won't teach anyone anything. None of the stories, fables, or verses in here has a moral. They're parodies. And while parody has often changed the course of history—a parody of a president, for example, brought Communism to its knees—these parodies have no such purpose other than to raise the odd chuckle.

The Book of Bad Virtues would not exist if Pocket had not thought of it, and I could not have produced it if they hadn't paid me a somewhat-smaller-than-Howard Stern-sized advance. Still, I can only hope someone somewhere takes as much pleasure and relish in it as I had writing it.

—Tony Hendra
September 1994 A.D.

I

CYNICISM

Cynicism—or giving up on life—is the first and most important Bad Virtue.

There are two reasons for cynicism: 1. Birth. 2. Death. No organism, from paramecium to parapsychologist, has ever succeeded in overcoming these two fundamental disorders.

In between is what we call life, a downward arc of brief expectations and lengthy disappointments. Life, Kahlil Gibran once said, is a lot like acne. It erupts one morning, bright and rosy, quickly reveals its true pus-filled nature, bursts, and scabs up. However often we pick at it, it scabs up anew. Finally, whether we go on picking at it or allow it to drop off of its own accord, floating away in minuscule fragments to join an atmosphere already heavy with the dust of countless other people's dandruff and acne scabs, it becomes a permanent disfiguring scar. No one, Gibran continued, with whom we wish to have hot, passionate sex can ever tear their eyes away from that scar.

From this we can deduce two things: First, given the huge worldwide increase in acne, dry scalp, seborrhea, and athlete's foot, the rainforest will soon choke to death on human skin. Second, Kahlil was not familiar with the modern American expedient of placing a shopping bag over the head of a person with whom you are having sex

3

and, as a further precaution, over your own. (A practice known to the *illuminati* as "double-bagging".)

For the last couple centuries, at least in the West, people have been gripped by an extraordinary mass delusion called Progress. Progressives believe, in the face of all the available evidence, that things get better as time goes on. Or alternatively, that life has a happy ending and that the Grim Reaper takes his bows along with the rest of us at the end of the comedy, cheated and defeated yet again. The Seven Ages of Man, in this odd philosophical construct, end at number Three or Four. What the Greeks called the Wheel of Fortune can, without tempting Fate, be safely made into a game show. In such rocky soil have sprouted a number of quasi-religions that hold, as one observer put it, that "death is an option." It's asserted, with confidence and without proof, that after two billion years of birth, decay, and death, a New Age is emerging— for some reason in northern California—when death will be little more than a speed bump on the driveway of eternal life. (New Agers have yet to address the simultaneous emergence of two hundred million handguns.)

Progress is coterminous with the embrace by western man of a religion called Technology. Techno-cardinals are more cautious than New Agers, asserting merely that with sufficient research death can be eradicated— probably by electrical means—and that decay is just a matter of faulty wiring. This optimistic proclamation is undercut by the fact that many techno-saints are currently, extremely dead.

Realism dictates not that technology has altered or even bettered the old familiar cycle, but simply that by lengthening the gap between birth and death, it has multiplied the occasions for disappointment. Unlike Aristotle, we now know that tires, as well as men, go bald.

Hope, we are taught, springs eternal; we are told less often that hope is a moron. Were the most basic tenet of Progress true, the planet would be swarming with incredibly old, incredibly healthy people, a few of whom would've been around for 100,000 years. Face it, it's not. People didn't get better all the time. They got worse. They keeled over in a field; they got impaled on pointed stakes by the guys downstream; they were swallowed by whales. Some fell down cracks in the Alps and froze. Others were run over by knights or spontaneously combusted.

Eternal life? They say the jury's out on that. Wrong. The jury's dead. Near-death experiences? Forget those too. Near-death is the same as near-pregnant. If the Intelligence Who Made It All really wanted to enjoy life everlasting with us, why did It create life non-everlasting? Why not just fast-track us to heaven and get on with the hallelujahs?

And if life is a Spiritual Aptitude Test, why wouldn't an Intelligence whom all faiths describe as Just and Merciful—and presumably Non-Sadistic—have given us some tiny clue that the test was worth taking? That eternity exists? Is *Embraced by the Light* as close as we get? If so, we're toast.

The truth is that the IWMIA birthed the universe and briefly had great expectations for it. Then It realized that nothing would ever again be as good as the Big Bang, that the universe was already—nanoseconds into its existence—a disappointing, anticlimactic, entropy-riddled pile of ever-cooling, ever more distant dirt, and that one day what It had created would be dead.

So It became the First Cynic.

Deteriorata

Go placidly amid the noise and waste, and remember what comfort there may be in owning a piece thereof. Avoid quiet & passive persons, unless you are in need of sleep. Rotate your tires. Speak glowingly of those greater than yourself & heed well their advice even though they be turkeys; know what to kiss & when. Consider that two wrongs never make a right—but that three do. Wherever possible put people on hold. Be comforted that in the face of all aridity & disillusionment & despite the changing fortunes of time, there is always money to be made in lawn maintenance. Remember the Alamo. Remember the *Pueblo*. Never forget that Mary Jo Kopechne was the savior of her country. Know yourself—if you need help, call TRW. Exercise caution in your daily affairs, especially with those closest to you—for example, that loser you sleep with. Be assured that a walk through the ocean of most souls would scarcely get your feet wet. Fall not in love therefore: it will stick to your face. Gracefully surrender the things of youth: red meat, elephant bells, drinkable tap water, LPs: & let not the sands of time get in your lunch. Hire people with hooks. Take heart amidst the deepening gloom that people in persistent vegetative states never have a nice day; & that whatever misfortune may be your lot, it could only be worse in Cleveland. You are a fluke of the universe; you have no right to be here, & whether you can hear it or not, the universe is laughing behind your back. Therefore make peace with your God, whatever you conceive him to be—Hairy Thunderer or Cosmic Muffin. With all its hopes, dreams, promises, & enterprise zones, the world continues to deteriorate.

Give up.

The Brilliant Bug of Carnegie Hall

In which we learn that the fire of artistic yearning can burn bright even within the tiniest exoskeleton.

Not very long ago, possibly as recently as last fall, there dwelt a bug in Carnegie Hall. He lived with his mother and slightly more than 181,000 siblings underneath the concert area over toward stage right. While his name need not concern us, he was a quite unique bug. Not in any outward way—for to all appearances he was just another of the millions of bugs who make their home in and around the huge bugopolis of the Carnegie. No, his uniqueness was within. He was filled with a burning ambition to be somebody. And since his frame of reference was the happenings around and above him, his ambition focused on becoming a really top-notch classical musician.

He applied for an appointment to see his mother, to get her advice on how to proceed. After several weeks his number came up, and he was ushered in to see her. (She couldn't, of course, allot him a big chunk of time since she had 7,330 more children to see that day.) He'd hardly got twenty seconds into his dream of becoming the first bug Yo-Yo Ma or Jean-Pierre Rampal when his mother interrupted him: "I've heard this crap before. You're a bug. Get used to it. Bugs don't play cello or flute, okay?

They scuttle blindly in dark corners looking for pathetic specks of food. You live, you die. Next!"

Now, the bug loved his mother and respected her opinion. But he was an American bug too, and he believed passionately that America, for all its faults, was truly the land of opportunity. No matter what people said, if you wanted something badly enough and you had the vision and stick-to-itiveness to see it through, you'd get your shot.

The bug enjoyed many instruments, but he felt the violin was king of them all. So he set about making himself a violin. Using his agile little forelegs and his fierce little mandibles, he painstakingly put together from tiny pieces of rosewood veneer an extraordinary instrument. It was very very tiny, of course, and you would've needed a microscope to see it. But if you had seen it, you could've sworn it was a Strad.

Next, he had to teach himself how to play. There was no teacher in all of the bugopolis, so he had to figure it out by himself. He happened to have perfect pitch, and the more he listened to visiting artists like Iona Brown and Itzhak Perlman, the more his proficiency and repertoire grew. But he decided to concentrate on getting one piece absolutely perfect. The piece he chose was Bach's Partita in D Minor for unaccompanied violin. After just a few months he could play a remarkably spirited interpretation.

He was ready to perform. Ready to perform at Carnegie Hall. How? Well, he'd figured that out too. Down by the footlights were ultrasensitive omnidirectional floor mikes that were turned on during singing recitals. He calculated that if he could get within a few millimeters of one of these and begin playing, the entire audience would be able to hear him. By crawling across the schedule in the lobby, he worked out when the next recital would be and began to practice in earnest.

The big night came. The house had filled up. It was that moment when everyone is starting to quiet down in anticipation of the performer's entrance. The bug knew this was his chance. He gripped his tiny violin and began to scuttle across the stage from under the curtain stage right.

The floor mike seemed so far away! And so big! But he was almost there, just a few feet more. The house-lights were going down. His timing was perfect! He reached the mike. He couldn't believe it! Could anyone now deny that America was the land of opportunity? He, a mere bug, was playing solo at Carnegie Hall!

He tucked his instrument underneath one mandible, raised his bow, concentrated for a long long second (just like Oistrakh used to), and began to play. The first tiny, haunting notes of the beloved partita soared through the auditorium, pure and sweet and perfect, the music of some infinitesimal sphere, sublime evidence of an intelligence that, however small, could bring genius to joyous life.

Then Kathleen Battle stepped on him.

The Boy Stood on the Burning Deck

AFTER MRS. HEMANS

> The boy stood on the burning deck
> And asked, with his dying breath,
> If things get better all the time,
> Then what the fuck is death?

Shit Happens

Folk Wisdom from the Great Religions of the World:

Taoism	Shit happens.
Confucianism	Confucius say, "Shit happens."
Hinduism	This shit has happened before.
Buddhism	This shit is not happening.
Zen Buddhism	What is the sound of one shit happening?
Islam	Shit happening is the will of Allah.
Judaism	Why does this shit always happen to *us*?
Protestantism	Shit only happens to somebody else!
Catholicism	Shit happens because you sinned!
New Age Thought	Shit is beautiful.

More Folk Wisdom from the Great Philosophers of the World:

Bertrand Russell	Define "shit"; define "happens."
Friedrich Nietzsche	Only the Ubermensch can make shit happen.
Jean-Paul Sartre	Hell is other people's shit happening.

Kierkegaard	Shit does not exist until it happens.
Immanuel Kant	Shit is a transcendental happening.
John Locke	Shit does not happen unless it is seen to happen.
St. Thomas Aquinas	Shit is defined by its happening.
Aristotle	Shit does not happen; it is caused to happen.
René Descartes	I shit, therefore I am.
The Stoics	Shit happens.

Leave It to Beaver

A FOLKTALE OF THE ARAPAHO

In which we learn that giving up can sometimes mean giving up on the false promise of progress, resisting pointless change—in other words, being a true conservative.

One day Beaver and Bear were walking along the river, when the Sun fell from the sky. It was not very large, about a handbreadth across, and perfectly round. It glowed bright yellow and gave off a great heat. Beaver, who was very wise, gave it wide berth. But Bear, who was very stupid, went right up to it and touched it.

"Ow!" he shouted. "It's so hot!" He thought for a moment. "Why don't we capture it?" he said. "And when winter comes, it will keep us warm!"

Beaver laughed in scorn. "You're so stupid, Bear," he said. "Haven't you ever heard of forest fires? The Sun will burn down our tepee just the way they do, and then how warm will we be?"

Sure enough, a spark jumped from the Sun into some branches, and they flared up. A little bird fell out of the branches, burned brown. Bear sniffed.

"That smells delicious!" cried Bear. "Why don't we tame the Sun and make it burn all our meat?"

"You moron!" said Beaver. "Everything we eat is fresh and pure. Our meat is dried by the clean, swift wind. Why would you want it burnt?"

Just then the Sun melted some stones, and they ran into a cleft in the rock and hardened. Out popped a shiny knife. Bear picked it up and felt the point.

"Think what we could do with a knife like this!" he cried. "It's so sharp! We could cut trees down and carve them into canoes and throw away our dumb old stone tools."

"You're such an idiot, Bear!" yelled Beaver. "Why would melted stone be better than stone itself?" He grabbed the shiny knife. "Here's the only thing this is good for," Beaver said, and cut off Bear's paw. Bear leapt around yelping in pain. Beaver had a good laugh.

Just then the Sun split in three. Two of the Suns began rolling down a slope. Bear forgot his bloody stump and watched them in wonder.

"Beaver!" he shouted. "Just think! If we put a stick between the two Suns, we could ride on it. We wouldn't have to walk ever again!"

Beaver shook his head in pity and contempt. "Only if you cut down all the trees and bushes!" he said. "Only if you flatten the mountains and beat special trails! You fool! It would be ten times more work than walking!"

Bear looked very stupid. "Well, perhaps we could put things on the stick and carry them around?" he said hopefully. Beaver looked at him. He didn't have to say anything.

Just then the first Sun cooled down and turned light brown and crispy. Beaver picked it up and sniffed it. He took a bite. "Delicious!" he said.

And that's how the tortilla came to be.

Lennon Lives!

An alternative to Giving Up is Wishing Things Were Otherwise. This little fable shows that even if They Were, you might still want to Give Up.

New York City. A wintry evening in early 1995. We are outside the Dakota on the Upper West Side. People are hurrying home from work along 72nd Street, coat collars drawn up to their freezing throats. The doorman in his little gatehouse by the forbidding entrance of the ultra-luxury building is hoping none of the Dakota's residents bothers him for a cab. It's cold out there.

Ah, shit. He can hear someone crashing out through the inner gate. Whoever it is is in a hurry, slamming the metal open, running toward the entrance. They're gonna want a cab.

He needn't worry. It's John Lennon, down from the vast apartment where he's lived now for a quarter century with his wife and son. Lennon, long recovered from the minor flesh wound inflicted on him by a deranged fan named Mark David Chapman, is fat-gutted, balding, what's left of his once-famous hair pulled back in a stringy, greasy ponytail. As usual, he's ranting.

He runs out through the arch and grabs a passerby by the arm, spinning the young guy round.

"You gotta gun, man? Everyone in New York's gotta gun, haven't they?"

The young man shakes him off. Lennon tries another and another. No good. An older, fiftyish guy stops.

"I gotta gun. Carry permit. Why, you in trouble? Hey, aren't you John Lennon?"

Lennon goes down on one knee, opens his arms.

"Shoot me, man! For Christ's sake shoot me! I can't stand her anymore! That fucking bitch is driving me insane! Twenty-five years of that fucking voice, those fucking stupid fucking shades. Kill me! Shoot me dead! Right fucking here and now! Please!"

The guy shrugs and walks off toward Columbus Avenue. The doorman pulls the door of his little gatehouse discreetly shut. Jesus. Every goddamn night. Embarrassing.

The Song of Doc Kevorkian

Times have changed. Dante put suicides in the Ninth, or worst, Circle of hell. Doctor Death puts them in the back of a 1968 VW camper, saying at the key point, "Have a nice trip!"

When you've multiple sclerosis
And you're hemophiliac,
Plus you're blind and black and homeless
—Call Doctor Jack.

When you find you're eating cat food
And Dad's had two heart attacks,
And even Spot's not looking good
—Call Doctor Jack.

When the bankers come foreclosing
And you're never in the black
And your T-bills take a hosing
—Call Doctor Jack.

When you feel profound self-pity
At the bottom of the pack
And life is, well, just *shitty*
—Call Doctor Jack.

When you're literally not yourself
Because you're on Prozac,
Nurse the real you back to health
—Call Doctor Jack.

When you're crashing from an interlude
Of crack and grass and smack
And the ATM says, "No way, dude"
—Call Doctor Jack.

When Dad won't give up the car keys
And Mom is on your back,
Plus your brother's being snarky,
Hey—call Doctor Jack.

When life is sweet in every sense,
When things are great, in fact,
Try a new experience:
—Call Doctor Jack.

The Fellow from Limerick

This important poem, by W. B. Yeats's brother U. B. Yeats, throws
open the whole question of nature versus nurture.

There once was a fellow from Limerick
Who was incapable of composing a limerick.
When asked why this was,
He said, "It's because
I was actually born several miles away in Cork,
And there isn't a rhyme scheme called a cork."

The Jogger Takes All

This story teaches us that there's a jogger in the pack, a joker in
the park, and that someday, somewhere we'll all run into him.

It was a bright and early mid-May morning in Central Park.
A spring day, a New York day, a hard-charging, nothing-
can-stop-us, step-aside-Buster day. The steel-and-glass
spires of the Manhattan skyline poked up through green-
dusted vegetation, as if stretching themselves toward the
sun. Many of the trees were still bare, but the cherries and
magnolias had exploded into cascades of pink and white
blossoms. From a distance it looked as if the park were
lined with giant pom-poms waiting to cheer the home
team on to certain victory.

Now, around the Central Park reservoir, as you little
cosmopolites must know, there is a jogging track on which
wealthy East Siders, and a smattering of prosperous West
Siders, strive to prolong their lives. It was too early for most
of them, being as yet twenty minutes till the *Today* show.

But toward the north curve of the track, where it almost reaches the 97th Street transverse, a lone jogger shuffled anticlockwise round the mere.

A sour note this fellow, upon so dazzling a cherry-blossom dawn. Dressed all in black he was, from top to toe, black Reeboks, black socks, black sweats, black hood drawn tight around his pasty, sickly face. Of course, as you all know from being dropped off in TriBeCa by your nannies to have dinner with Mom and her new boyfriend, there's nothing special about basic black. New Yorkers of all ages and genders have a taste for widow's weeds, not so much because they're mourning the demise of Something Big as because they're too darn busy to count calories. But it's rare upon the jogging track. There, those who pass the hours of work and play in funereal hue prefer colors that make them look like the offspring of Arlecchino and a large parrot.

So it was with the hearty chap who now disembouched upon the track from its 90th Street entrance. A stout brigantine of ample tonnage, this runner, topping two meters without his size 12 Nikes, parti-colored tights of Day-Glo green and red stuffed like bright sausages by his oak-thick thighs, a vast warm-up jacket in blinding purple and orange highlit by silvery reflectors billowing over his splendid belly, a yellow Walkman strapped to beefy biceps and wired to ursine ear, twixt fiery red ponytail and chest-length beard. John Henry was his name.

Thumping north along the dirt with a tread that surely shivered the timbers of the Guggenheim and made IVs sway in Mount Sinai, John Henry soon drew abreast of the dark one, and *Hi*-ed him cheerily.

Death—for, as you smart little whippets have already guessed, Death it was who trudged so painfully along the fence—gave him a sickly half-smile and turned back to his punishing task.

"You okay?" roars John Henry, brows like a fox's brush bristling with concern.

"Sure," wheezes Death.

"Want to run with me a ways? Easier with someone to chat to."

"Be my guest."

"I'm John Henry."

"I know."

"You know?" squints John Henry, incredulous, happy as a Brobdingnagian bivalve. "How come? 'Dja see me on HBO?"

"Could be, think so, yeah."

"HOW ABOUT THAT!" bellows the brightly colored one, proffering a high-five the size of a garden fork. Death flaps back at it, his hand a weary flounder. They run a few steps with disparate gait, John Henry waving that great mane from side to side in glorious disbelief.

"So—what's your name?"

"Call me Mort."

"Been running long?"

"Just started."

"Tough at first. Gets easier, though. No pain, no gain, right, Morty?"

Whereupon the large fellow slaps his companion between those thin shoulders and sets off a hacking, snorting, coughing fit, like an old Ford pickup trying to stay alive on one cylinder. John Henry stops, his hamburger-red forehead wrinkled with care.

"You sure you wanna go on, Mort? Hey—we don't want you going south on us, do we?"

"Never happen."

"Sure. That's what they all say. This young guy runs the Mannyhanny ten-K the other day? Older fella collapses in front of him. Young guy doesn't BREAK STRIDE! Steps right over him. He's laughing, for Christ's sake. Like the old guy deserves to croak."

They start to jog again, John Henry restraining his fustian legs to a trot, Death with a shuffle that hardly clears the dirt.

"So a hundred yards further on, the young guy keels over too. Stone dead. Massive coronary. Thirty-seven years old!"

"Yeah, I know."

"You ran that ten-K?" Incredulous, but in his way, well-mannered, John Henry avoids the obvious question—Did you finish? Little ears, take note. Good manners are never out of style.

"No. But I was there. Terrible."

Now the Dark Angel gets into a true tussle with his lungs. The coughing's so bad he has to support himself with one limp claw entwined through the cyclone fence around the reservoir. John Henry puts hammy fists to hips. "You're giving it up, pal. This ain't your day. Let's get you a taxi."

"I'm fine." He's hacking like a mule in heat. "Things been slow lately. You sit around, you smoke too much."

"Ain't that the truth."

Death is adamant. One lap at least. John Henry frowns, but off they set again, black Reeboks hobbling behind life-boat-size Nikes.

"What you do?"

"Disposal."

"Waste disposal?"

"Kinda . . ."

"Locally?"

"I get around. Been doing a lotta work overseas."

"Yeah, where?"

"Europe. Africa. Haiti. Can we stop talking now?"

Performing more than one physical task simultaneously—running and talking, for example—is hard for folks who smoke three packs a day, even if they're immortal.

"Sure. Like I say, for me it helps keep your mind offa the agony."

Several quiet moments pass. John Henry is beginning to puff a little too, toting all that freight. Now, perhaps for the first time, he examines his new friend as they lumber along. The thin sloping shoulders, the weird all-black outfit, the cowled head held forward and just a little to one side. Why does a chill of recognition zip up John Henry's spine?

"You know," says the friendly Barney-man, "I can't get over feeling I've met you someplace."

"You have never seen me before."

Death shoots a glance at John Henry. No more pasty face. Deep in the cowl, a skull grins out at him, its dead white bone untouched by sunlight. Then he turns back to running. John Henry skids to a halt, grabs the thin shoulders, spins the Dark One round.

But the pasty, sickly puss is back, sweating in the hood. Not a pretty sight, but that's warm spit on those lips. The skull is gone. (Isn't this goose-bumpy, kids?)

"Hey!" yells Death. "Quit that!"

"Wait a minute. Wait just one frigging minute. You know me . . . Mort . . . saw the guy at the ten-K . . . disposal . . . You can't be . . . I don't believe it! I gotta tell someone! Hey, you!"—to a macaw-colored matron pounding by—"Lookit this, willya! A celebrity!"

"Shut the hell up, man. I'm on my break."

"Oh, yeah? Death takes a break, huh?"

The Grim Reaper resumes his hobble-de-hobble along the track.

John Henry watches him for a moment, stroking that bale of red hair on his face, unsure for the first time in decades what to say or do. Then he lets in the clutch and steams up alongside. "I must be going nuts. I'm jogging round the fucking reservoir with Death."

Nothing from Death but puffety-puff. The little angel that could.

"Steve and the guys put you up to this? Howdya do that Skeletor bit? You ain't really Death, are ya?"

"Well, I ain't Christopher Plummer."

"How come you're in such shitty shape? What happened to Death the All-Powerful?"

"Told you. Smoke too much. Overweight. Can't keep up?"

"Why? AIDS? Drive-by shootings?"

"Peanuts. Less than peanuts. There's one and a half billion more people than there were twenty years ago. Forget Rwanda, forget Bosnia—drops in the bucket. Plus, this whole health kick's killing me."

A big speech for the little guy with lung trouble. It's Chloraseptic time again. The hacking's worse than ever, but does John Henry care now? Oh, no. He's got a grin splitting that shrubbery as wide as all get-out.

"I guess so! I guess we're finally giving you a run for your money, huh?"

Death is bent double. He's out of answers. He's leaving the track, folks! He's heading for the grass!

"Know something, douchebag? Two years ago, before I started taking care of myself, I would've been scared shit-less of running into you. But now—lookit ya! Hey—I bet you that in my lifetime the boys in white coats are going to come up with something that just about puts you the hell outa business!"

"Could . . . be . . ."

Uh-oh. A cold front is about to meet the warm front. Severe storm watch in the tri-state area!

"WAIT! WAIT! I get it! This is the classic trap, right? I get overconfident, then *WHAM!* Right when I least expect it—you do me!"

The Gentle Giant is mad now. He picks the hacking, spewing Dark One up by the scruff of his sweats and sticks his vast face an inch from mortality.

"RIGHT?"

Death nods weakly. John Henry shakes him the way

the super shakes a garbage bag to get the used diapers to the bottom. "You gonna do it to me, pal?"

"Not . . . exactly . . ."

The brawny lad's eyes widen to the size and color of Pizza Hut Pan Pizzas. He lifts Death up with one fist, so tight he can't even cough, so high those black Reeboks swing clear of the chlorophyll.

"Just one fucking moment, pal. What the fuck is 'NOT EXACTLY'? IS THAT A THREAT? No one, but no one threatens John Henry Johnson, Jr., on the streets of New York City! *COMPRENDE?*"

The hood lolls back and forth. Could be a no, it could be a yes. The human thunderstorm drops the garbage back down on the grass. He snorts a great snort of something— triumph, contempt, revenge, who knows? John Henry is done.

At this point, my little ones, a very odd thing happened. Listen carefully for there may be a pop quiz at the end of my tale.

Death lay where he'd been dropped, on his back, his chest heaving. Suddenly he grabbed it—his chest—and arched his back. He grunted, loud, like the first part of an elephant trumpeting, and slumped back. The pasty, sickly face began to melt away into the hood. For one brief moment there was the skull, dull deadbone laughing at the sky. Then it was gone, and Death's body too. The sweats went flat like a big pool toy when it springs a leak. And that was that.

John Henry watched the miracle with bulging orbs. Up came another jogger—a little squirrel of a woman with oversize spectacles and Nikes to match.

"Oh! I'm sorry. I thought it was someone lying on the ground. But it's just a pile of clothes I guess . . ."

John Henry Johnson, Jr., had nothing to say to little squirrel people. He flung his purple and orange arms in the air. He spun around, a one-man carousel of color. He whirled up through the thickening trickle of joggers coming down the runners' lane on the Central Park Drive.

"Death is fucking DEAD! And I did it! Me! John Henry Johnson, Junior, from Jackson City, Missouri! You know what this means, people! Do you KNOW what this MEANS?"

He twirled a tall blond woman round like a Barbie doll. He hi-fived two WASPY cockatoos. He clapped a black lawyer from Paul Weiss on the back and sent him sprawling. He turned a huge kaleidoscopic cartwheel in the middle of the road.

And what do you think happened then, dear children? Can you guess, my little Manhattan meanies, my little NYC cynics? Well, possibly not. The ambulance that came speeding round the corner just as he finished his cartwheel missed him. And the seriously deranged homeless guy who stuck a dirty needle in him on his way home turned out not to be HIV-positive.

Next day he blew a weekend flight to Nantucket from La Guardia by minutes. It nose-dived into Long Island Sound, killing everyone on board. Walking down East 92nd Street one week later, he stopped to tie his shoe on the stoop of a brownstone and half its cornice fell exactly where he would've been if he hadn't stopped. The same day, a drunk rear-ended his vintage Mustang on I-95 at about seventy, slamming him into an abutment and turning both cars into fireballs. The drunk was incinerated. John Henry walked away.

Then he disappeared. Vanished from the face of the earth. Went out running one morning—never came back. No warning, no message, no suicide note, nothing. Not a trace of John Henry Johnson, Junior, was ever found—except his jogging gear, lying in an untidy heap beside the Central Park Drive.

II

DISOBEDIENCE

It all begins with parents. In an age when everything that was once considered an inexorable fate can now be changed—sex, nationality, cup size—parents remain fixed, the North and South poles of our world, the plus and minus terminals on our life's car battery.

Parents are your fate. Their biology is your destiny. Their DNA is your jug ears, your pimples, your heart attack. And no matter how hard you fight destiny—by changing your sex, nationality, or cup size—your parents will still be there, squinting at you as you get out of the car at Thanksgiving, their glasses skewed and slipping down those ugly beaks they bequeathed to you, saying, "What *did* you do to your nose? Is that a ring?"

Of course we love our parents, sorta, kinda, most of the time, but it's a biological love, a love that knows no name, a love that doesn't use enough mouthwash.

There is nothing in life so difficult as raising children, yet no one requires parents to have an iota of training to accomplish it. To hunt, drive, practice law, or engage in any other blood sport, you need a license. Not parents.

Parents betray you. The five or six longest years of your life are between the time you become fully conscious, around the age of three—when you stop being little more than a large, wet, ambulatory vegetable—and the moment you get your first Game Boy. During this

27

period your parents are the Zeus and Hera of your universe, yet they blithely go to work or restaurants or ball games or the toilet or, even, in some cases, Mexico. Do they consult you? Never. An hour is a day to you, a day a lifetime, but after waiting for Zeus and Hera for a lifetime, you're lucky to get a quick squeeze while their godlike eyes are glued to Peter Jennings.

Worse still, they may even split your universe in two by introducing into it, without your approval, another you. Not only is this person entitled to fifty percent of all your galaxies, quasars, black holes, etc., but for the foreseeable future you are stuck with them. They bawl, you get the time-out. Or if you are the introducee, you acquire willy-nilly a president-for-life; you're condemned forever to play second fiddle, be someone else's gofer, outfielder, and heavy bag.

Why on earth, therefore, would parents command or even expect obedience? What could be more natural than to ignore everything they present as desirable or wise? Particularly when you are beginning to realize that Zeus would never pull those few pathetic strands of graying, greasy hair into a ponytail, and Hera would definitely get rid of that ghastly wen-thing on her chin.

The term *dysfunctional* as applied to families is negative; it presumes the existence of the word "functional" in this context. The word exists, but there has never been a family to which it could be applied. Dysfunction is the norm in human families, and disobedience, active or contemplated, is its glue. Disobedience is the door to the secret garden, a ticket to the bliss of first love, the bond of Tom and Huck, a knife through the apron strings, the catcher in the rye.

There is something ominous about obedient children: boys who keep their cubbies neat without being sweepingly threatened, girls who say "please" when no substantial incentive has been mentioned. Observers assume that, behind closed doors, physical abuse must be involved or that someday the little angel will snap and Kill Five. Charles Whitman was an Eagle Scout; William Calley was "always there" for his classmates.

For children there is nothing improving about the traditional—i.e. Victorian—notion of obedience. It springs from the myth that kids are squeaky-clean little vessels waiting to be filled by the wisdom of their elders, when in reality, they're hot little cauldrons filled to the brim with bubbling hormonal menudo. Obedience is just a delaying tactic used by parents to keep the lid on the pot until the inescapable day it boils over. Then disobedience, the natural condition, takes control.

The Frog Prince

FROM THE BROTHERS DIMM

The story of the Frog Prince is one of the best-known fairy stories
of all time. The burden of this story is supposed to be that
children should keep their word. But it also illustrates the
truth—well known to women—that most men are moronic,
unfeeling horny reptiles.

*The story of the Frog Prince goes like this: A beautiful young
princess drops her gold ball down a well by mistake, and
an ugly frog gets it back for her on the following conditions:
to wit, that she promises to love him, to have him for her
playfellow and companion, to let him have dinner with her,
to eat from her plate, to drink from her cup, and to sleep in
her little bed. She agrees to it all, he retrieves the gold ball,
then she reneges and runs off. Next day the frog shows up at
dinner demanding his half of the deal. The beautiful young
princess consults her wise father:*

"That which thou hast promised thou must perform
always," said her father the king colorfully.

So the little princess, who was so lovely that the very
sun stopped in its circuit of the heavens to wonder at her
beauty, opened the door and let the big, fat, slimy old
frog inside.

The frog, dripping the most disgusting excrescences
from its horny back—for a broken septic line leaked into
the well, and its fecal coliform count was sky-high—
jumped up beside the princess and flicked his tongue at
her. Some of its spit hit her face. She shuddered, but at
least, she thought, the horrid thing's staying in its own
chair.

31

Fat chance, lovely little princess! Suddenly the amorous amphibian leapt with one bound into her lap. It looked up at her with bulging eyes. "Feed me, sweetie," it said.

So she did. The frog slurped down everything she put in its mouth. It licked her fingers, leaving a kind of stinky cheeselike residue on them. It demanded a straw and sucked down at least a liter and a half of red wine. It ate an entire duck with damson plum sauce. It insisted on several desserts, sitting in one of them—a syllabub—and taking a mud bath in it. Every time the princess moaned at the horror and loathsomeness of it all, her father remonstrated with her.

"Do thou be faithful to thy word withal, for thou art of right royal blood," he said in his inimitable fashion.

"Why?" sobbed the princess. "The damn thing did me one small favor. I've repaid it just by letting it in the door. When . . . will . . . this . . . end!"

The frog finished what was left of the crème brûlée and jumped back into her lap. Then it threw up.

"Oh, God!" she screamed. Jumping up, she tried to wipe the glistening heap of frog vomit from her pretty crinoline, but it stuck to the silk in a glutinous lump. The frog fell on the floor, clearly smashed out of its mind.

"I feel better now!" it said. "Let's hit the sack."

"Nononononononono!" the lovely girl sobbed. "Please, Daddy, don't make me!" But the king her father grew angry, saying, "That which thou pledgest in time of thy necessity must be performed to the utmost of thy strength."

So the poor thing, who it must be remembered was only fifteen, had to pick up the still heaving frog and take him to her bedchamber. She threw him in a corner, where he immediately went to sleep. The princess changed into a sweet-smelling teddy-style nightgown, threw the sick-covered crinoline out the door for the maids to take care of, and jumped into bed.

Of course, she couldn't catch a wink. The reptilian reprobate snored in the corner, belching and farting in its sleep.

Eventually she dropped off. No sooner had those long lashes closed over those lovely eyes than the frog was on her pillow.

"Gimme a kiss," it slurred, and the stinky cheese stuff dripped from the corner of its floppy mouth.

"Never!" she whimpered, "never in a million years!"

But the frog kissed her anyway.

Instantly it turned into a horribly obese young prince who was losing his hair. Like the frog, he was drunk and had no clothes on. There was dried vomit at the corners of his mouth. He began slobbering all over her, giving her hickeys. The beautiful young princess shrieked and struggled to get out of bed. But the drunk blimp prince had other ideas. With a grunt he rolled the soft grublike folds of his belly over on her legs, pinning her. Then he began trying to work her teddy up over her head.

Suddenly the door of the bedchamber flew open. There stood her father, with several armed guards.

"O wanton child!" thundered the sovereign. "Have you no shame? Not content to resist the obligations you have incurred, must you now drag our royal name through the pigsty of lust?!"

The fat prince lumbered up off the princess and stood on the bed, swaying. Then he belched, long and loud, right in the king's face. Purple with rage, the king grabbed for him, but at that moment he turned back into a frog and jumped out of the window, never more to be seen.

The beautiful little princess pleaded with her father, desperately trying to explain what had happened when he made her take the frog to her bedchamber. But he turned a deaf ear and ordered the guards to throw her into a dungeon.

The next day, the king publicly disowned his daughter in the marketplace of his capital, causing her finery to be torn from her body and replaced with sackcloth rags. She was then shoved unceremoniously out of the main gate of the city, under a royal decree of perpetual banishment. Later, she came to America and worked for many years as a ticket clerk on the Erie-Lackawanna Railroad.

———

Kate Who Would Not Eat Her Soup

AFTER HEINRICH HOFFMANN

This cautionary rhyme is for parents, not their children. Its message is simple: Kids know best.

In Croydon, hard by Londontown,
There dwelt a girl of small renown
—And lamentably low estate—
Who answered to the name of Kate.

Her parents, as perhaps you've guessed,
Financially were somewhat pressed,
Resorting frequently to soup—
A source of tension in the group,
For Kate, while of angelic mien,
Malingered at the old tureen.

No matter how her dad waxed wroth,
Kate would not, ever, eat her broth.
Variety did not entice:
Minestrone, bouillabaisse,
Mulligatawny, borscht, or chowder
Absolutely nothing wowed her;
Present the perfect waterzooie
Her sole reaction would be "Phooey!"
Be it gumbo or cioppino,
Kate would murmur—"Not for me, no."

Before too long, needless to say,
Young Kate began to waste away.
Her worried mum worked twice as hard
To keep her well supplied with lard
And jam and shepherd's pie—all dishes
British gourmets find delicious.
No good. Kate shunned such nourishment.
The wicked girl was adamant.
"You'll die," sobbed Mum, "as sure as eggs.
Or else have really dreadful legs."
But nothing moved the stone-faced Kate,
Her rosebud mouth was obdurate.
And even if some wayward crumb
Found lodging in Kate's sunken tum,
Off to the loo she'd skip alone—
And call Ralph on the Big White Phone.

While siblings swelled, their sister shrank,
With no one but herself to thank.
Some felt her high school photos forced
Comparisons to the Holocaust.
Her legs and arms and face—so thin!
The rest a tube of bone and skin.

Had I to find one word for it—
The little hoyden looked like sh-t.

At this point parents might incline
Toward a tale that underlined
The certain, swift, and hideous fate
Awaiting kids who act like Kate.
The facts of modern life we face,
Alas! do not support this case:
More often children's wickedness
Will earn them staggering success.

Ironically, a fast food chain
Gave Kate her first keen taste of fame.
A photog for the fashion ads—
Who liked his lasses more like lads—
Espied young Kate's puerile hips
While savoring some egg and chips.
He looked her up, he looked her down.
No female contour could be found—
No fat, no curves, no soft sweet bumps.
He loved, he said, her lack of rumps.
Whence Kate—in finance far from naif—
Consented to become his waif.
Her hungry please-don't-feed-me face
A hundred magazines soon graced.
And now the chicken-legged gamine
Went everywhere by limousine.

Meanwhile, across the ocean broad,
A grand designing man, long bored
By hourglass figures, was obsessed
By one so very genderless.
This fellow's taste was quite advanced.

passing kind to him; she taught him his letters and changed his Underthings when he was caught Short. Yet had she one custom by which the boy was mightily Repuls'd; whenever he might have a Smudge on his face or neck, as after he had broken his fast with bread and Marmalade, he might have a Spot of Jam stuck upon his lip, then Granny would take out her silken handkerchief and hawk a Gob of Spit into it, and therewith wipe the Smudge or Spot away. And if there were more than One, or it were stubborn, she would repeat the hawking, rubbing more Slimy Stinking Gobs on Willie's visage, till she were like to bathe the poor boy in Spit. There, she quoth, thou'rt clean betimes; albeit Willie's skin crackl'd with dried Slime and stank like the rotting toothless gums of the old Crone.

Willie thus was cleft by the horns of a Dilemma. He was a dutiful Grandson withal, according his dear father's mother the respect due our Elders and Betters. Yet was he cognizant that honorable Men do not lightly suffer Gobs of Spit upon their Person. Young Willie was thereby forced to Exercise his Conscience without benefit of Superior guidance, of which task he acquitted himself most worthily. One day he crept to his father's chamber at dawn, where having secreted in his hosiery his dear parent's choicest dirk, he went to breakfast. After they had broke fast, Granny, as was her wont, sallied forth with Willie into the garden. It chanced that a daub of Marmalade yet bedew'd Willie's chin. This Granny espied, and taking out her silken handkerchief, she hawked therein a mighty Gob of Spit like a Football, and bent over the boy to clean him. Whereupon Willie drew the dirk and stuck it in his Granny's Nostril, and compelled her backwards until her Bonnet caught on an Apple

Bough. Then he slit her from Gizzard to Guts like a Hog on a Hook. And who can blame the unfortunate Childe?

MORAL
Whether on Silk or Skin 'tis Spill'd
Spit is Spit and Grounds to Kill.

———

The Woodsman and His Hairy Daughters

FROM THE BROTHERS DIMM

German fairy tales are a standard part of any collection of acceptable children's stories. What they're supposed to teach children, however, is anyone's guess—unless the kids happen to be neo-Nazi skinheads.

There was a poor woodsman who had three buxom daughters of marriageable age, all of whom were quite hairy. The youngest had a moustache, the middle one had a beard, and the eldest had a moustache and a beard. The woodsman, who could neither afford to feed three buxom young women, nor had the wherewithal to provide any of them with a dowry, was at his wit's end as to what to do to get them husbands. For what man in his right senses wants a hairy bride?

One night a wicked elf came to him in a dream. "I can get your daughters husbands with the power of my magic," said the wicked elf. "The first day, take the youngest deep into the forest and nail her to a tree by her lips. During the night I will cause her moustache to vanish, and at dawn a handsome young gentleman will appear who will rescue her and, by so doing, fall in love and marry her. On the second day, take your second daughter to the same spot and nail her to the same tree by her chin. During the night I will make her beard vanish, and at dawn a handsome young prince will happen by, rescue her, and fall in love also. On the third day, do likewise with your eldest daughter, nail her by her head to the tree; during the night I will cause all her unsightly hair to vanish, along will come a fine young king who will rescue her and fall in love and marry her as the other two have done.''

The woodsman was overjoyed that his daughters would get such fine husbands, yet asked he: What must I do in return? Each time you go into the dark forest with a daughter, said the wicked elf, you must leave on your threshold a poisoned herring.

The next morning the woodsman explained his dream to his daughters. So delighted were they at the prospect of such fine husbands, they deemed it a small price to pay that they would have to stay all night in the dark forest nailed to a tree.

That very day at twilight the woodsman took his youngest daughter and, having left a poisoned herring on his doorstep, led her deep into the forest. There he found a mighty linden tree. Placing her hairy face against its trunk, he hammered a long iron spike through her lips and nailed them tight to the tree. Blood and bone and tooth and gristle splattered the bark, but hope shone in his daughter's eyes, and she smiled as best she could. The woodsman returned home with a light step.

When he arrived at the door of his hut, the poisoned herring was gone, but upon the roof was a dead badger with a ring of amber round its neck. Trembling with fear, the woodsman went to sleep. *(In some versions he now becomes a loaf of enchanted bread—Ed.)* That very night a second wicked elf came to him in a dream. "I am the first wicked elf's twin brother," said the second wicked elf, "and I bring bad tidings. Before the handsome young gentleman could come at dawn, the Witch of Esalen, disguised as a gray wolf, tore your daughter from the linden tree. Only her lips remain. When you take your second daughter to be nailed to the tree tonight, hearken well to what the lips tell you, or she, too, will be lost."

The next day at twilight, the woodsman took his second daughter by the hand and led her deep into the forest until they reached the linden tree. Leaving her a little way off, he approached the tree. Sure enough there were the lips of his youngest daughter still nailed to the bark, caked with gore and a few bloody entrails torn from her neck. The lips began to speak:

> Kiss me, Father, kiss me true,
> Kiss me hard what-e'er you do.
> If you don't kiss me ere you leave,
> My dearest sister soon will grieve.

So the poor woodsman kissed the bloody lips long and hard, and they turned into an owl, which flew upon a bough. Realizing that his second daughter would now be safe, he drew her to the linden and, placing her hairy face tenderly against the trunk, hammered a mighty iron spike through her chin and nailed it fast. Again blood and tooth and bone and gristle flew all over the bark, but his daughter's eyes shone bright with hope, and she smiled as best she could. With a light step the woodsman returned home.

Alas, when he got to his hut, the dead badger on the roof with an amber ring round its neck had changed into an adder with two heads. On the other hand, the poisoned herring was back on the doorstep! Trembling with fear, the woodsman retired to bed. *(In Hauptmann-Gault, significantly, the woodsman is now devoured by a small toad—Ed.)* That night in a dream, a third wicked elf came to him. "I am the first and second wicked elf twins' twin brother," he said, "and I bring sad tidings. Before the handsome young prince could come with the dawn, the Warlock of Waldheim, in the shape of a great raven, killed the owl which you thought had the magical power to protect your second daughter but did not because you omitted to leave a second poisoned herring on the threshold. The great raven tore your daughter from the linden tree. Only her chin remains. Hearken well to what the chin says when you take your last daughter to be nailed to the tree, or all will be lost."

Cursing his stupidity, the woodsman took his third daughter the very next day at twilight into the dark forest, leaving two more poisoned herrings on his doorstep beside the first, together with a loaf of enchanted bread. When they reached the linden tree, he left his daughter a little way off and approached the tree. Sure enough, there was the chin of his second daughter, caked with blood and shattered teeth, the tongue black and swollen, nailed fast to the trunk. The chin began to speak:

> Punch me, Father, punch me true,
> Punch me hard what-e'er you do.
> For if you do not punch me well,
> My sister soon will dwell in hell.

So the poor woodsman smote his daughter's bloody chin with a mighty blow. It flew from the tree and became a rolled-up hedgehog with poisoned quills. Knowing this was a good omen, the woodsman drew his last daughter to the linden and placed her hair-covered face against the trunk. "You are my last and dearest," quoth he, "but this time all is well." Then he kissed her tenderly and hammered a mighty iron spike through her head and nailed it fast.

Instantly her body flew apart into a thousand pieces, leaving only the severed head spinning on its nail, spouting blood. "Fool!" cackled the severed head as it spun, "we are not your daughters but goblins come to take your soul to Hades."

Immediately the woodsman, invoking the name of the adder's second head, became a bear and, catching up the hedgehog, threw it in the air, whereupon it became a woodpecker and pecked out the eyes of the head, which spat out the lips of the first daughter, which ordered the thousand pieces of the third daughter's body to dance forevermore. Meanwhile, the bear became a wild duck and flew away with the poisoned herring, and the severed head ate itself. *(In the Bavarian version the bear is either omitted or is Jewish—Ed.)*

MORAL
Germans, despite a reputation for being logical and orderly, are just as confused as the rest of us.

The Story of Abraham and Isaac

GENESIS 22

The beloved tale of Abraham's devotion to his heavenly Father is here told in its unadulterated, most ancient form. Tradition has it that the story was first written down by Isaac himself.

And they came to the place God had told him of; and Abraham built an altar there, and laid the wood in order, and bound Isaac his son, and laid him on the altar on the wood. And Abraham stretched forth his hand, and took the knife to slay his son.

And Isaac said in a loud voice, Father, art thou full of nuts? Gettest thou that thing away from me.

And Abraham answered, saying: The Lord thy God came unto me saying, Take now thine only son Isaac and get thee to the land of Moriah and offer him there for a burnt offering upon one of the mountains which I will tell thee of. And behold this is that mountain.

And Isaac said, That beeth it? The Lord thy God told thee? Wherefore did the Lord my God not tell *me*? What am I—liver that hath been chopped?

And Abraham said, Thou art my only son *Isaac,* whom I love; when I slay thee the Lord God will know I fear him above all others. And Abraham stretched forth his hand once more and took the knife to slay Isaac.

And Isaac said, How dost thou know the voice thou hearest in thy pate beeth the Lord God? For lo according to my mother Sarah, thou art at least one hundred and fourteen years old. It is not the Lord thy God that speaketh to thee, Father, but something thou hast eaten rumbling in thy ancient bowels. Thou shouldst lay off the figs and goat cheese.

And Abraham said, The Lord God has spoken. And Abraham stretched forth his hand yet again to take the knife to slay Isaac.

And Isaac waxed exceeding wrath and said in a great voice, Thy faith giveth thee the power to dispose of thy loved ones like a dirty pot? It is not the Lord God who speaketh to thee but the bats which inhabit thy belfry. And will I prove that thou art naught but an old fool, for lo, thou canst not even tie a decent knot.

And Isaac sprang from his bonds the which he had loosed, and took Abraham and bound him and laid him on the wood. Then stretched he forth his hand to take the knife and slay his father.

And Abraham was greatly afeared and babbled in strange tongues and soiled himself. Whereat Isaac took pity on him. And the two of them went down out of the land of Moriah together.

Then did Abraham come privily unto the scribes, saying that the Lord God had spoken to him at the place of burnt offering and praised his great devotion and released him from the sacrifice of his beloved son Isaac. And that moreover, Abraham's seed should be as the stars of the heavens because he had obeyed His Master's Voice.

And the scribes wrote down whatsoever Abraham told them, that it might promote righteousness and *Family Values*. Yet what manner of father looketh to score points with the Lord God by killing his only son?

The Perfect Mother

C. Z. LEWIS

From the moment we're conceived our mothers shape us: they teach us to toddle, to talk, to read, to think and feel and love . . . When you think about it, it's completely ridiculous—as this delightful story spells out.

Oh, how the children loved their mother! She was not like other mothers. She wore her thick blond hair in flowing tresses or—when she was in her studio—in a large loose chignon. Her clothes were loose and flowing too, full-length skirts and dresses of heavy material, richly embroidered, that fell in thick folds. She loved dresses with trains, which she would cinch high under her bosom in the manner of the ladies in Renaissance paintings. Sometimes, on special occasions, she would even put on her wedding dress with its acres of lacy train, then, holding it in one hand, dance a saraband for her delighted children.

Maeve, the youngest, actually believed that her mother was a fairy queen, who could work spells and talk to other fairies. And certainly at their Midsummer Night party, perhaps the most important feast of their year, Mother did like to be called Queen Mab. Maeve even swore to her brother and sister that one late spring evening, looking down from the wisteria-framed window of her bedroom into the rose garden below, she had seen diaphanous fairy wings sprouting from Mother's back.

And then there were the fairy rings. Quite often in the early morning, when the dew still sparkled on the spiderwebs, their mother would take them down to the meadow. There in the tall grass they would find a rough ring of toadstools, sometimes oval, sometimes squarish, sometimes almost perfectly circular. Around the ring, the grass would be a little crushed, as if tiny feet had danced upon it, or tiny bodies had rested there. And even if, like Miranda, who was almost eight, you only half-believed it anymore, there was this magical feeling hovering over the ring that not long before someone had been there. And Mother was uncanny when it came to fairy rings. She always seemed to know exactly where to find them.

Had their father really been an ogre? Their mother said he'd been a handsome prince when first they met, but that the prince's wicked stepmother had cast a spell that turned him into a dreadful ogre who stood eleven feet tall in his stockinged feet. She said he had eaten their baby brother one day for breakfast and as a punishment was doomed to live forevermore in a horrid, sunless, barren land of dark mountains. Parsifal, the eldest, had a faint memory of an enormous man with a booming voice. Sometimes the man was reaching up for him in a mighty oak tree, and sometimes he was sitting at a table laughing at what looked like a huge roasted bird, which sort of matched up with the pictures of ogres he'd seen. But Mother said they were just bad dreams. They never ate roasted bird—or any other animals for that matter— and never had. Besides the ogre that used to be his father had a great black beard. But Parsifal did wonder why something in a bad dream made him feel so warm and sad. Secretly he vowed that when he was old enough he'd travel to the dark horrid land, find the ogre, and kill him. Or perhaps he'd become an ogre too. He hadn't decided yet.

One of the things the children loved about their

mother was that they didn't have to go to school. Their
mother taught them at home in their big rambling farm-
house—when she wasn't too busy casting spells or sew-
ing tapestries. They didn't have to do boring stuff like
math and geography either; she taught them songs and
folk remedies and ancient crafts.

But best of all they loved the stories. Their mother
was always reading them stories. There were stories of
gods and sea voyagers and gladiators, of knights and
damsels in distress, of dragons and trolls and witches
and pixies and djinns. There were terrible names in
many of the stories, which crackled or thundered or
hissed when their mother said them. Some of the stories
rhymed and some were in funny language that made Parsifal and Miranda laugh. But Mother didn't like the children to laugh at her stories. They were supposed to listen
attentively, or they'd have to go down to the dungeon for
a while.

It was quite amazing how many of the stories were
about children to whom the most terrible things happened. One day Parsifal asked his mother why. She said
all the stories had lessons to tell and that even when the
children didn't seem to be naughty, they were often doing something bad, such as being lazy or greedy or rash
or ignorant or talking out of turn. The very best way to
learn about life was to read and reread the old stories,
even if they were written thousands of years ago, because
modern man had lost his way in a forest of facts and no
longer had a sense of the world's magic.

Mother became very beautiful when she said things
like this. She would get up from wherever she was sitting
and glide over to the fire or an open window. The only
sound was the rustle of her dress on the carpet. Then she
would stare for a while into the flames or at the trees

outside and repeat the last thing she said. The room became very quiet as if it were full of invisible listeners listening to her words and agreeing with them. Miranda said it gave her the most delicious goosebumps.

But this one time, Parsifal really didn't understand. They had been reading "Hansel and Gretel" that morning. How did that teach Parsifal, Miranda, and Maeve anything? he asked. They didn't have a wicked stepmother, you couldn't build a house out of cookies, and there were no such things as witches.

"Really?" said his mother, smiling that mysterious smile that Parsifal knew made her look very lovely but somehow made his tummy bunch up.

Parsifal admitted he might be wrong about witches; but still, he said, does "Hansel and Gretel" mean it's all right to kill them? (Secretly he liked the killing-the-witch part, but he couldn't believe this was the lesson of the story.) His mother replied that no, it was never right to kill anyone or anything, but that that wasn't quite the point.

There was a long silence. Parsifal racked his brains for a point, but nothing came. His mother smiled again and said that "Hansel and Gretel" was about a sister helping her brother, about courage and resourcefulness in the face of great danger.

Parsifal thought about that. So it was all right for someone to kill a witch so long as she was helping her brother. Then he thought of the resourceful Hansel leaving a trail of breadcrumbs on the forest path to find his way back. Of course birds would eat the crumbs!—or mice or squirrels or groundhogs, for that matter. Hansel was a moron.

He mentioned this to his mother—though more tentatively than he thought it. Mother didn't like the m-word.

"Well, what would you do if someone wicked took you deep into a dark forest?" she asked.

"Carry a cellular," said Parsifal.

So he had to go down to the dungeon for a while.

On the weekends the children had no lessons. Often friends of their mother would come to visit. They were all women. On Saturday nights, the children were allowed to stay up for dinner with Mother—and with her guests if she had some staying. They loved to hear the grown-ups talk, for it was almost always of wonderful things, such as starships and ancient cities and pyramids and spirits and magic and angels and amazing things that people could do and that were going to happen.

How did the children and their mother live? By magic, of course! Whenever they needed money, Mother spun some gold from her magic loom. They had a fairy carriage, but Mother didn't like to drive, so it sat in the stable waiting for a ball to take them to. Sometimes the lights would go out for a few days. Then they cooked in the great fireplace in the dining room, just like the knights of old. They had a big vegetable garden, but there were trolls in it who blighted all the plants and fruit trees; Mother grew her magic herbs there though, and that kept the trolls in line. Sometimes they went roaming in the woods and the fields, picking things for dinner— mushrooms, hickory nuts, watercress, wild blueberries, and, once, acorns.

And even if, as happened every once in a very long while, they grew tired of watercress sandwiches, or Mother's magic loom refused to spin some gold, there was always her father, the king.

The children's grandfather was king of the north

country, where he lived in a castle by the sea. They visited him once in a while, often for their favorite feast of Midsummer. He was a tall, thin old monarch who lived alone, having survived, so Mother said, all his courtiers and the knights who rode with him in days of yore. While he wore no crown, his castle was built of stone and full of cavernous, drafty rooms. Its mighty walls, which boasted the requisite turrets, arrow-slits, and crenellations, stood on a bluff that swept down to the rocky shore of the northern ocean.

And so it was that the children and their mother came to be sitting that Midsummer Night below the castle walls overlooking the ocean. Not long before, in the garden of the castle, they had performed their Midsummer revel for the king. The revel, which Mother had adapted from many sources, was led by her, as Queen Mab, in a splendiferous full-length gown of filmy materials, interwoven with garlands of flowers and boughs, while crowning her glorious hair was a charming pre-Raphaelite coronet laden with more flowers and from which trailed silks and gold trimmings.

Miranda and Maeve were wood nymphs, attired in short diaphanous gowns of many colors, whose various pieces were designed to resemble petals. Parsifal was dressed in parti-colored doublet and hose. The revel required him to change headpieces several times, including an ass's head his mother had woven from sisal and which pricked and tickled his face like nobody's business! There had been much dancing and madrigals sung to a lute that Mother played with bittersweet simplicity. Now it was time to pay their respects to the Goddess of the Moon.

The ocean was uncharacteristically calm under the hot June night. The moon shone down from the clear, star-sprinkled sky, its light creating the most extraordinary effect on the water—a bright wide silver path stretching from the rocks on the shore to the horizon. It was the highway to the land of make-believe, said Mother, and she had a keen desire to see where it might lead.

The children watched rapt as their mother walked slowly down the slope to where the highway began. They could hardly believe that the vision gliding down to the ocean before their eyes was their mother—was even mortal. Her long, shimmering gown caught in the gentle breeze, the moonlight stippling it with silver and glinting off the golden highlights of her crown. The loose drapery and silken darts of her costume stirred around her like the fronds of some fabulously exotic underwater plant or the trailing clouds of otherworldly light that swirl around a Tiepolo angel.

The children watched as she stepped from rock to rock until she reached the very edge of the silvery path. And, miracle of miracles, they watched as she now trod on the silvery path itself, moving out upon the water as her slippered feet found substance there. Surely she was, as Maeve had always believed, a fairy queen!

Farther out she moved, one delicate, languorous step at a time. Now she was indisputably, impossibly, *magically* walking down the moon's broad road toward the land of make-believe. The children watched as the majestic figure paused in that slow way she had, her gown and costume stirred again to gossamer life by the sea breeze, and turned back to wave at them, their fairy mother, their queen of bright magic.

And the children watched as she now slipped off the submerged rocks she'd been treading on and fell into the water. The children watched as she sank into the re-

markably deep gap between the rocks and then rose
again to the surface, her gown tangling around her as she
fought to get a grip on the rocks.

"Silly bastard," said Parsifal.

Miranda and Maeve looked at him in utter shock.

"You said a b-word," said Maeve.

"I'm going to have to tell Mother," said Miranda.

"Go ahead," said Parsifal.

They looked down at their mother, whose head and
shoulders were now moving rapidly out to sea, along the
moon's silver highway, dragged by a fierce riptide. She
was trying to wave her arms, but they were hopelessly
entangled by tentacles of sopping silk and crepe. Faint
cries were borne on the offshore breeze.

"We really should call someone," said Miranda.

"Yes," said Parsifal. "We really should."

III

GREED

We need greed. Greed makes the world go round. Greed drives history. The greedy fish wriggled up onto shore, looking for more, and its greedy spawn grew feet and arms and waddled about looking greedily for food, becoming in the fullness of time Rush Limbaugh.

But the kind, caring, compassionate, self-denying fish who stayed behind, sharing their portion of the primeval pudding with crustaceans less fortunate than themselves, are forgotten, lost in the spume of history, anonymous grains of sand upon a beach in Pensacola. Heed well their sad end, Bill Moyers.

Without greed no Great Pyramid of Cheops, no tomb of Diocletian, no Mayan temples, no Golden hordes, no *Niña,* no *Pinta,* no *Santa Maria,* no Manifest Destiny, no MTV. Greed moves mountains, building affordable town houses where once there was but tumbleweed. Greed mines the wealth of nations, greed weaves the fabric of society, greed lubricates the cogs of self-interest, greed breeds discipline and good manners and *pretty please with sugar on it.* Greed founds religious orders, greed speeds missionaries to martyrdom, greed caters charity lunches, greed creates the homeless and the kitchens for their soup. On greed feed parasites such as think tanks, coalitions, citizen action groups, Centers for This and That; greed pumps good dollars after bad into querulous quarterlies and meretricious monthlies. Greed hosts weekend retreats, conferences in Aspen, Institutes for Heavy Thinking, Club Meds for the head. Greed provides the paneling, the snow-white linen, the heavy silver, the obsequious illegal aliens that make it possible for neo-Augustans to sit around deep into the night waffling about Virtue.

The Goose That Laid the Golden Eggs

FROM TALES BY ASSOP

In which we learn that greed, coupled with the right technology, works wonders.

A man and his wife had the good fortune to own a goose that laid a golden egg every day. The eggs varied slightly in quality, from around fourteen karats to around eighteen karats. They varied even more in weight, depending on the thickness of the shell. (The eggs were not, as many assumed, solid.) Some days the egg might weigh as much as eight or nine ounces, sometimes as little as three. Depending on the daily price fixing in London, which at that time fluctuated considerably between a low of about $210 an ounce to a high of around $326, this could mean extraordinary instability in their monthly income—or rather that of Acme Precious Metal Inc., the Delaware corporation through which they traded.

Seeking to both maximize and stabilize their cash flow, the man and his wife decided to find out more about the internal physiology of the goose. They reasoned that it was possible the goose was composed entirely of gold. Since the animal weighed almost twenty pounds this could give them a one-time capital infusion, which had some advantages over an unpredictable revenue flow, especially in the light of Acme's rising costs (e.g., processing the impure metal, brokers' commissions, etc.).

They hired a reputable veterinarian who took the goose to his clinic, placed it under general anesthetic, and made a large incision from the bird's sternum all the way to the base of its vertebrae, thus exposing the ovarian tract. He was not surprised to find that its internal anatomy was entirely normal. The man and his wife, however, were taken aback and demanded that the veterinarian perform a more invasive procedure, specifically on the ovarian tract. He refused unless they agreed to sign a waiver freeing him from all liability in the event that this had catastrophic consequences (e.g., trauma to the reproductive system, which might prevent it from laying any further eggs).

OPTIONAL MORAL ENDING A: While they were discussing the waiver, the bird experienced acute respiratory failure and died. Thus the man and his wife neither achieved a one-time capital infusion, nor did they any longer have a monthly income. They brought a malpractice suit against the anesthesiologist, but it was thrown out of court.

OPTIONAL MORAL ENDING B: The veterinarian convinced the man and his wife that the risks of a more invasive procedure far outweighed the benefits. He closed and sutured the incision. After a week or so, the goose recuperated and began again to lay the golden eggs. Acme continued to experience erratic revenue flow but later diversified into municipal bonds and achieved a measure of financial stability.

OPTIONAL MORAL ENDING C: The man and his wife signed the waiver, and the veterinarian proceeded to examine the bird's reproductive system more closely. He found that the golden eggs had actually occluded the bird's ovarian tract and that nine fully formed normal eggs were thus prevented from being laid. He removed the eggs, closed the incisions, and placed the normal eggs in an incubator. The goose recovered fully and resumed laying golden eggs. All nine normal eggs hatched successfully, and at an early age the goslings also began to lay golden eggs. For unexplained reasons the quality of the gold improved to a fairly consistent twenty-one karats, and sheer volume ironed out the peaks and valleys in the egg-weight curve. Through regular cesarean section of the normal eggs, the flock of geese grew to number some 1,200 birds. Acme Precious Metal experienced an annual growth in excess of one thousand percent for seven straight years, went public, doubled its stock several times, and made the man and his wife incredibly wealthy.

————

The Story of Midas

This retelling of the ancient legend of a fabulously wealthy king underlines the importance of more stringent handgun control.

There was this guy called Midas. Not a king, just an ordinary Joe. He lived in Los Cerritos, with his overweight teenage daughter Marianne.

Midas was a nice enough guy, except he was always dreaming about getting rich quick. Various schemes had come his way, and he'd made a little on some of them, but nothing spectacular. His wife left him when he got involved with Amway, which she said was a cult. Then she started drinking, so Marianne came to live in Los Cerritos. She worked at Burger King once; now she watched TV.

One day Midas was in the den checking the lottery

numbers, when a shadow fell across him. Looking up, he saw a stranger dressed in shining white, smiling down at him.

"Holy shit!" said Midas, diving for the Beretta he kept in the drawer.

"Hold on a second, Midas," said the stranger. "I bring you good news."

"Fuck you, asshole," said Midas and shot him in the throat. The stranger slumped to the ground, mortally wounded. Blood spurted from his carotid artery, like water from a garden hose.

"You fool!" said the stranger. "I was going to give you the power, starting tomorrow, of turning everything you touched into gold."

"Yeah, right," said Midas, dialing 911, "and I'm the fucking Queen of England."

Midas got off with justifiable homicide. Sometimes of an evening though, he wondered about the stranger in shining white and what it would be like to have that power. Just think—he could turn his fat fucking daughter into gold, melt her down, and buy a boat. Pay off the house too.

Oh, well.

From *Poor Richard's Almanac of Modern Wisdom:*

Early to bed, early to rise, makes a man healthy, wealthy, and utterly despised.

An Amusing and Improving Tale

The 1980s, when the solid, trustworthy values of the 1880s began to return in earnest to American life, offer us countless inspiring tales; happily, they also brought us other things our forebears of a hundred years ago knew little of.

There was once a financier called Mike. Mike was the very essence of what makes great countries great. He worked hard, he played for keeps, he took chances, he pushed the envelope, and he wasn't afraid to make tough decisions. He did not shrink from the truth that the weak and underachieving are doomed and that the strong survive. Above all, he was constantly and restlessly looking for ways to grow, to expand, to move in on the next guy. When opportunities presented themselves, he moved like lightning to take advantage of them, multiplying his fortune to extraordinary levels in the process.

Before long Mike was one of the wealthiest men in the land. In one year alone he made $550 million. Associates calculated conservatively that he was worth well in excess of a billion dollars, but other interests he built up, warrants and so on, could have doubled or tripled that amount. He encountered opposition, as all strong men do, and was forced to pay a huge fine to the government for various supposed infractions of the rules—about $600 million by the time it was all over. Still he remained a staggeringly wealthy man; it would have been only a matter of time before he restarted, undoubtedly to become once again a one-man symbol of economic strength and initiative.

Unfortunately something else was growing and expanding, constantly and restlessly, and it was inside Mike. It was engaging in a hostile takeover of his subsidiaries. It moved like lightning to take advantage of Mike, multiplying itself in the process to the level where it became, . . . excuse me . . . inoperable. And by . . . the time you . . . ahem! . . . read this, Mike . . . oh dear . . . will . . . be . . . hee hee heee! HAHAHAHAHOHO! O GOD! THAT'S F- . . . I'm sorry, I'm sorry . . . OK? Try again.

By the time you read this, Mike will be dead.

Christ — The Early Years

BY REV. RUPERT SHULA

Little is known of Christ's first thirty years. If the Rev. Shula is right, however, his youth exemplified the Calvinist belief that God rewards virtue with prosperity and that the poor have only themselves to blame.

Jesus went to school in Jerusalem and got excellent grades. This was no surprise for the Lad was industrious, hardworking, and keen. Jesus had to walk to Jerusalem every day, for there was no transportation to school, nor did the Christs expect any. One night He didn't come home, nor the next, nor the next. Perplexed, his "parents" set out to find Him. Imagine their surprise when they got to Jerusalem and there was Jesus sitting in school, surrounded by His teachers! Mary went up to their "son" and asked Him what He was doing. Prophetically the Stripling replied:

"Don't you know that I must be about my Father's

business? And that the business of my Father *is* business?"

When Jesus said "Father," he meant God, of course. Mary, on the other hand, thought He meant Joseph, which was hardly surprising when you consider that she had met God only once, many years before and for a very short while. But her mistake gave her a great idea.

Why not send Jesus to college? Not only would this give Him all the advantages higher education can bring in later life, but He could learn advanced skills and help Joseph in his struggling carpentry business.

Her "husband" and "son" agreed enthusiastically, and before long Jesus was a familiar sight on the bustling campus of Galilee Community College. Knowing the sacrifices Joseph and Mary were making, Jesus studied hard at His minor, Advanced Carpentry, and His major, Business Administration. (Although the true love of the tall, strapping, blond, young Son of God was sports.)

One fateful day during summer vacation, Jesus was sitting in Joseph's carpentry shop, whittling away at a wooden peg. The peg, when completed, would be used to connect two boards into which Joseph was laboriously boring holes. Suddenly the younger Man threw down His work.

"Dad," he exclaimed, "I've got a great idea!"

"Fire away, 'son,' " rejoined his father distractedly.

"Metal's harder than wood, right?" demanded Jesus. He hurried on impatiently. "So if we sharpened a small piece of metal, we could bang it into the wood without boring holes. And if we banged it through two pieces of wood, they'd hold together, wouldn't they?"

He seized the two boards from the carpenter's unwilling hands and turned His words into deeds. He handed the result to His skeptical onlooker. The two boards seemed to be tightly fastened by the sharpened piece of metal. Would they hold? They did! Try as he could the grizzled craftsman could not pry them asunder. Jesus had invented nails!

Nails were the turning point for the Christ family. Thanks to his business training, Jesus knew that it was not enough to have a good idea. In order to maximize its potential, you must promote it aggressively. Nails cut Joseph's production time in half, enabling him to move up delivery schedules and beat out the competition. Orders poured in. More, in fact, than Joseph could handle. But did Jesus turn them down? Of course not. He saw growth, He saw *expansion*. Why not, said Jesus, open a whole chain of carpentry shops with a reliable image and exclusive rights to nails, then lease them to independent contractors for a fixed monthly fee?

All they needed was a catchy name. One morning Joseph noticed that the sign outside his shop, "J. Christ & Son Carpenters," had been taken down. In its place was a colorful new sign, showing Jesus and Joseph in carpenters' aprons. Above their heads was the proud legend:

TWO GUYS FROM NAZARETH

Enterprising carpenters, anxious to get their hands on nails, bought into Jesus' idea in a big way. Throughout Galilee "Two Guys from Nazareth" signs mushroomed overnight. Of course, Jesus and Joseph weren't actually working in the shops—they never had to lift a hammer again. But they sold all the nails, cut an exclusive deal with a hammer manufacturer for "Two Guys from Nazareth" hammers, and got their fixed monthly fees. All that remained was to hire a reliable security firm that investigated complaints, collected unpaid bills, and had "friendly chats" with anyone inclined to pirate the nail idea. Jesus had both revolutionized carpentry and invented franchising!

———

The Hamilton Philadelphia Letter

Alexander Hamilton, father of the American economy, predated M. W. Kiplinger by some hundred and fifty years. His confidential business report was circulated to all men "of good sense and mercantile zeal" from 1776 until Hamilton's untimely death. This issue was mailed the day after the Constitution was signed.

CIRCULATED WEEKLY TO BUSINESS CLIENTS SINCE 1781—SEPTEMBER 18TH, 1787

Honorable Sir,

Our New Constitution is a Godsend to Merchants, Bankers, Planters, and all Others dedicated to Property and Increase.

The "Fellows in Philly" have not forgot on which side their bread is buttered: In all questions of *taxes* and *commerce* our Government is to be Supreme . . . in all questions of *"rights,"* however, the fledgling Constitution, like our beloved President, hath no teeth.

"The Red White and Blue Menace of Democracy hath been destroyed Utterly," Framers say in private. Attention of Convention was successfully kept off radical nonsense and upon business, tariffs, regulation of commerce, etcetera.

Absence of Patrick Henry, weakness of George Mason and other radicals helped . . . as did foresight of President

Washington in sending *Mad Tom Jefferson* to Paris as Ambassador. Jefferson could have swayed Convention to accept *Bill of Rights,* which Constitution doth not include . . . yet. New England nay-sayers and even some Middle Colonies may insist upon it before ratification . . . business interests going to work on state delegates with despatch . . . *usual friendly persuasion.*

Even if Bill passes, the imp may yet be exorcised . . . Framers have drawn up such a Bill secretly, avoiding all talk of franchise, abolition, and so on, which should shut up the Loud-Mouths.

Point of Interest: The Bill would also guaranty *Right to Counsel* at government expense. The more than half of the Framers that are lawyers thus put *A Tidy Piece of Business* in their own way . . . a good augury.

Meanwhile Constitution makes few concessions to the Separatists . . . States retain control over some matters but nothing considerable. Most powers will stay with the Central government . . . means money for *Gifts, Consulting Fees, Wenches, Jaunts, etcetera, will be more efficaciously spent.*

Herewith how the Johnny-Cake crumbleth:

No King, alas, but . . . President hath Vast Powers. He will be chosen by men of Property, merchants, bankers, or planters called Electors. This ensures *permanent control of the Presidency by commerce* and quick disposal of Presidents who chuse to march out of Step. In addition, size of Continent will require Presidents to spend heavily to make themselves known . . . Money is not going to come from tinkers, farmers, and other small beer.

No standing militia, yet . . . but formation of Navy dandy. We spy formidable gravy from government in *Ship*

Building, Tar, Timber, Hardtack, Cannon, Cotton, and Whip-Leather.

Wherefore Slavery? Permitted until 1808 . . . Men of sense at the Convention realize this gives those who find it Useful more than *Twenty Years* to unhorse the silly Prohibition. Meantime *runaways and other human chattel* must be returned to their rightful owners.

Publication of Congressional Debates is required only at the discretion of Congress . . . another neat handstand. Secrecy not of massive import since business rarely contracted in the chambers of government but rather in privacy of feasts and estates . . .

Checks and balances may appear hostile . . . and could be if some cantankerous voice is raised in Congress. Yet they render *Government so cumbersome* that commerce can be in and out and have its breeches buttoned before they can call the Constable.

The absurd Proposal that debts be cancelled . . . was foreclosed upon without delay. *Shay and his ilk* will henceforth be consigned to the Poorhouse. There are yet *some in Philadelphia who prefer no government at all* as the road to prosperity . . . Framers are reminding these good people that *only one-half of one of three branches of government is to be Elected* and that by Men of Property only . . . that no member of Congress may be arrested while he is about the business of government and that Congress is required to meet but one day in the year . . . and then in the dead of Winter.

All in all, they confide, *the Constitution is designed to be used when necessary, ignored when not.*

Election of Mr. Washington bears this out . . . Although the Continental Congress and new order require President to be elected, Convention simply by-passed the law and appointed him "unanimously."

What then can men of Worth and Good Sense expect?

We foresee colossal investment possibilities, new construction of *Mighty National Tariff Walls, The Subsidization of Private Property with Publique funds, and the elimination of unnecessary competition* . . . not to mention the garnering of citizens' money into huge *"National Banks."* Indeed, a popular jest today in Philadelphia is that Mr. Washington will no longer be casting silver dollars from the Banks of the Delaware, he will be casting them *for* the Banks of Delaware!

The prohibition upon states raising tariffs against their fellow-patriots is most important . . . The novelty of the unchartered corporation seems destined to a hugeness equalled only by nations themselves . . . Further, people may now be sold things they never dreamed of . . . exempli gratia: codfish to the Carolinas or watermelons to Vermonters . . . provided only that they can be persuaded to want them.

Transport of these luxuries will become paramount . . . due to the vast distances involved . . . Look for *weighty profits from Ships, Wagons, Carriages, yea, Anything with Wheels.*

More important still: absence of Regulation. How important this may be is demonstrated by an example of "fraud."

Many grocers and butchers are wont to wrap their produce in bright paper by a given weight and adorn it with some fancy name . . . though it costs them but a farthing, the novelty causeth customers to swoon and they may charge twice as much as before. Thus the tradesman increases his cost by next to nothing, yet causes his volume to soar . . . and all at the customer's expense . . . With this principle applied to all manner of commerce and disseminated throughout the Republic without regulation, fortunes may be made Overnight.

Most important of all: formation of the Republic would place all the immense territories of the states at the disposal of the central government . . . The fortunes to be realized through *enlightened speculation in land* hath no limit . . . Several Proposals were made during the course of the Convention to name the Republic, *The United Real Estates of America.*

Should the Constitution then be ratified?

Aye, says President Washington . . . Attempts at this pass to remove unpleasant morsels will only arouse the radicals, proffering them an issue to exploit. Washington himself hath instructed all fellow Freemasons to vote yea on threat of expulsion.

Mood amongst the Framers is that *the Constitution represents a victory over the Revolutionaries and their excesses* . . . The hot heads who have rogered the country so savagely since the war's end have been given the old Boot.

As for the rabble . . . Leaders feel that common folk have done their part in separating us from the unprofitable tyranny of the British . . . Now they must be awakened from their silly dream of power . . . notwithstanding which they can swiftly become the best market ever known to mercantilist man.

As Mr. John Jay put it aptly: Those who own the country ought to govern it . . . Our understanding is that those who own the country consider they have shared it quite long enough with those who merely inhabit it.

If ratification is forthcoming, the future of commerce looks bright. The joint mind of Framers is best conveyed by a quip of Mr. Ben Franklin at a banquet following last night's announcement of the Constitution. A common woman approached him and asked, "Well, Mr. Franklin, what do we have—a Monarchy or a Republic?" To which Mr. Franklin replied, "You, madam, have nothing. We have a Republic—if we can keep it."

I remain
Your obedient Servant,

Alexander Hamilton

Sept 17th 1787   The Philadelphia Hamilton Editors

IV

SLACKING

Work is obsolete.

Three generations ago men and women still worked. Men dug coal in holes with picks made of steel other men had dug from other holes. In shipyards more men riveted ships together to carry the coal to mills to smelt the steel other ships carried back to the shipyards to make more ships. Farmers spent their lives on tractors growing food to feed the men in tractor factories or cotton to clothe the women in clothing factories or tobacco to steady the nerves of chemists making chemicals to grow the food, cotton, and tobacco. Loggers hacked down forests ships carried to kraft mills to make the paper for other loggers' pink slips. Roughnecks drilled oil to fill trucks with fuel for assembly lines where autoworkers made the pickups roughnecks needed to drive to the rigs to drill more oil.

And so on. Everyone helping one another, relying on one another, trusting their fellow proletarians to do a great job, sweating and toiling in an interlocking daisy chain of mutual futility that need never have existed if all the participants had simply made the decision to shove it. Don't drill oil; you don't need a pickup and your brother in the one big union doesn't have to build it. Stay out of holes—no coal to smelt the steel to make the pick to dig the coal. Simple.

Deep down all workers understand that most work is make-work. Its only beneficiaries are those who don't work: the very rich and the very poor. Idleness is everyone's goal. (The failure of socialism wasn't due to the Soviets' corruption or the Pentagon's courage in outspending them; it lay in Marx's idiotic assumption that workers actually like working.)

The post-war generation took a giant step toward idleness by figuring out that almost everything their parents had sweated and toiled over could be committed to paper. The actual tasks—digging, drilling, hacking, hauling, etc.—since they were ultimately futile, could be consigned to disposable people, preferably abroad. The new generation would become executives. So now men and women spent their days making photocopies of forms requesting requisition orders for service reports to be filled out when their copiers were serviced or distributing memos calling meetings to discuss spreadsheets of sales figures of paper companies who specialized in spreadsheets and memos. The apple never falls far from the tree.

Vast tracts of idleness were opened up. Old-fashioned tangible idleness, like whittling sticks or sitting on your back porch spitting, which went along with tangible work, was replaced by the intangible idleness of television. At the same time, television assuaged people who felt guilty about their idleness by allowing them to spend it watching other people work—or pretend to. (Actors are the only people our society currently permits to call their idleness work.)

The current generation, however, has taken the greatest step yet by consigning all work to cyberspace. This has transformed the work-idleness equation. For one thing it makes work completely intangible. You can't even experience the vestigial satisfaction there was in moving a tower of paper from the In basket to the Out. Whatever you've accomplished is hidden out there, in the unforgiving darkness behind the screen saver. The paper generation is unemployed and unemployable, their jobs dissolved into the same darkness, never to be retrieved. And consigning work to cyberspace blurs the work-idleness distinction irreversibly. We spend all day looking at a screen and all night too. Media conglomerates profit from either kind of viewing. They manufacture the entertainment that drives our idleness, and they own the screens on which we work by day. Some people even use those screens to speculate in the stock of media conglomerates. Is speculating in idleness work? Which is more entertaining—the Disney Channel or Disney stock when Eisner's having a bad day?

As consolidation continues, as more and more people are controlled by fewer and fewer pairs of eyes, as we have more and more time to fulfill more and more of our needs through the looking glass of the screen, our idleness will become essential to the economy. Were we not to purchase by modem the CD-ROM about breaking into the computer networks of global media conglomerates we saw on television in a scene from that pay-per-view movie about hackers produced by a global media conglomerate, the country would collapse. We will depend on one another's idleness, avoiding sweat and toil, in the same daisy chain of mutual futility that once made the smokestacks belch. Work will be more than obsolete. It'll offend the Anglo-Saxon idleness ethic, not to mention Rupert Murdoch and SkyMart (a division of FoxMicro-Bell). So be a responsible hard-idling citizen. Stay home and slack so America can stand tall again.

The Song of Gorging Wolf

A FOLKTALE OF THE KASKA

One of the most prominent personages of the Kaska tribe was a
kind of anti-shaman charged with keeping things light—the
ancient version, perhaps, of late-night talk-show hosts. Gorging
Wolf would have been one of these (known literally in Lakota as
Boy-Who-Talks-Funny).

We hunt the buffalo in the spring,
Said Gorging Wolf.
We pick the chokeberries in the fall,
Said Gorging Wolf.
In winter we sleep,
Said Gorging Wolf.
We are happy.

Those other ones, the cornheads,
Said Gorging Wolf,
They are soft from their corn.
Said Gorging Wolf,
Their men are like women from no hunting.
Their women are like men from too much eating,
Said Gorging Wolf.
They are not happy.

If we want their corn, we will take it,
Said Gorging Wolf.
Rip it from their soft hands and eat it,
Said Gorging Wolf.
We will kill their men and rape their women,

Said Gorging Wolf.
Or perhaps the other way round.
Gorging Wolf smiled.
It will be easy,
Said Gorging Wolf.
We will be happy.

Some day we, too, shall die,
Said Gorging Wolf.
Return to the Great Spirit in the sky,
Said Gorging Wolf.
After many moons men shall come,
Said Gorging Wolf.
Men with soft hands and minds,
Said Gorging Wolf.
And they will look at what little we left behind,
Said Gorging Wolf.
A few bones, some stolen scraps of cloth, an arrowhead,
Said Gorging Wolf.
And wonder at our glorious legacy,
Said Gorging Wolf,
Sing praises of us as the most perfect of men,
We shiftless wanderers, we happy parasites.
Gorging Wolf smiled.
And our shades shall look down upon the soft men
And laugh their asses off.

The Little Tin Soldier

BY HANS CHRISTIAN COALITION

Idleness includes shirking—and one of the most important things
we should shirk is duty, officialdom's oldest and cruelest hoax.
This beautiful story underlines the futility of dutility.

There were once two dozen tin soldiers. All were brothers, because they had been made in the same mold from
the same chunk of metal. Oh, were they smart looking!
They had red tunics and white pantaloons and blue and
silver shakos, and each held a bayonet. Stiff and proud
they stood, the very model of military splendor.

For many years the tin soldiers traveled widely. They
fought in numerous battles, and even when they fell, they
held themselves upright, bayonets firmly on their shoulders, shakos firmly on their heads, ready for the next
skirmish. They lived together in a wooden box, which
over time became quite battered and discolored. Over
time so did the tin soldiers. Several bayonets got bent;
hands and feet went missing. Worst of all, three of the
brothers were lost in various places, never to be found.
But did the others display an iota of emotion at these
tragedies? No, of course not.

One day they were put in the box and left alone for a
very long time. No one took them out; no one even shook
the box, as they had done in the old days, to feel their
heft. But they never complained. They just lay in their
box staring straight ahead, gripping their weapons, ready
to fight when called upon. So it went on for many years.

Finally they felt themselves being picked up and

handed from one set of hands to another. Then, for the first time in all those years, they heard the box being opened. Looking down at them was a heavyset man in a Lacoste T-shirt. He had the big jowls and fleshy face of someone who liked his food and drink, but it was his eyes that caught their attention. They stared ahead, fierce and unblinking. His eyes were the eyes of the tin soldiers.

The big man took one of the brothers from the box and put him on a table. He happened to have lost a leg, this particular tin soldier, as well as the tip of his bayonet; nonetheless, he stood as stiff as ever, shako tight upon his tin head, the very model of a military man. The man brought his white-haired head down to the level of the table and stared deep into the tin soldier's eyes. Then he saluted him.

The tin soldiers were happy to be back with someone who appreciated them. After a few days, they felt themselves being moved. Then they heard the rustling of paper. The next thing was the words: "Tin soldiers?" The words were spoken by a little boy who didn't frankly seem that thrilled to see them. But did that bother them? No, sir, not one whit!

The little boy's father was the big man who had rescued them. He set the tin soldiers out on the table, arranging them in a squad. There were four ranks of five soldiers each.

Battered and chipped and faded though they were, they looked splendid in formation. The little boy's father was having a splendid time too. He adjusted one of the corner men, who was very slightly out of alignment, and began explaining the details to his son: the parts of the bayonet, the vintage of the uniforms, the origin of the shape of the shakos. When he'd finished, he smiled a rare smile.

"What d'you think, mister?"

"Dad . . . I wanted . . . P-P-Power Rangers."

Under his breath the little boy's father muttered, "Le-e-e-ft turn!" Then he turned each one of the soldiers ninety degrees to the left. The obedient tin soldiers did whatever was asked of them, ever upright, tin eyes fixed on their duty.

And what of the one tin soldier? He stood upright too, on his one tin leg, ready to serve as well. Certainly he had no part in the squad for now, but that was just the whim of his commander. His tin bayonet was ready, his tin tunic was uncreased, his fierce tin eyes awaited his assignment.

Just then the one tin soldier caught sight of a G.I. Joe on a shelf in the little boy's bedroom. He was the bravest looking toy soldier the tin soldier had ever seen. His beautiful helmeted head was thrust keenly forward, searching for the enemy. His muscular body gleamed bronze. His manly fists clutched a huge weapon the tin soldier had never seen before but which he knew to be mighty and powerful. Best of all, the G.I. Joe had only one leg. The little boy had pulled off his left leg months before because he didn't like G.I. Joes, but the tin soldier would never know that. All he knew was that he had found a kindred one-legged spirit. Love flooded his tin heart. Ah, if only he could mount to the shelf—that unattainable balcony so high above him—take the beautiful, brave, bronze G.I. Joe in his arms, and give him a big tin kiss!

Nothing of his love showed on the tin soldier's face. He stared ahead, bayonet on shoulder, as dedicated and impassive as the day he was forged. As if to reward his constancy, the little boy's father picked him up and placed him at the head of the squad. He was platoon commander! He wondered if the G.I. Joe had noticed his promotion, but the hunky peg leg was ever alert, his sharp eyes scouring his surroundings for trouble, far above the tin soldier's shako.

The little boy's father got up from the table and put his arm round the little boy's mother. He gazed down at his son, who in turn was gazing miserably down at the tin soldiers.

"See? Just like I told you. He loves them," said the little boy's father.

"Yes, Bill," said the little boy's mother.

When it was time for supper, the little boy was ordered to put the tin soldiers back in their box. Being a good little boy, he did as he was told—all except for the tin soldier with one leg. Him he knocked over and left lying on the table. But the tin soldier didn't mind. From where he lay he could stare at the G.I. Joe all night and perhaps even figure out a way to make his acquaintance.

That night, when all the people in the building had gone to bed, the toys held a party. Most all the toys in the nursery were wonderfully old-fashioned for the little boy's father loved old-fashioned things. There was a top that you pumped and which hummed as it rotated. There was a music box that played "The Battle Hymn of the Republic." There was a penny bank with three Negroes playing baseball and a rocking horse and a marionette theater. The music box turned itself on, and all the toys danced and jumped about in the most amusing way. The only ones who did not move from their places were the little tin soldier and the G.I. Joe. The G.I. Joe stood on his shelf, keeping watch over the nursery, while the little tin soldier lay on his back at attention, never taking his eyes from the intrepid infantryman.

Twelve o'clock struck—*crash!*—on the grandfather clock by the door. Up sprang the lid of an old wicker hamper and out popped a wicked black golliwog.

"Yo, Tin Soldier," said the golliwog, "keep thine eyes to thyself. Gaze not on boody thou canst never possess!"

But the tin soldier pretended not to hear.

"Uh-huh," said the golliwog. "Just thou waitest!"

For quite some time after that not much happened. Every night, when he was not attending to affairs of state, the little boy's father would come to the nursery and show the little boy how to play with the tin soldiers. Whenever his work took him far away, he would call the little boy's mother to see if his son was playing with the tin soldiers. And the little boy's mother made sure he did.

When neither of his parents was around, the little boy made the tin soldiers spin through the air like ninjas and kick one another in the head. He'd line up five of them—he called them Trini and Billy and Zack and so on, just like the Power Rangers—while the rest would be the evil forces of Rita Repulsa. Then the Power Rangers would kick and zap and laser the bad guys into submission. If he heard his father or mother coming upstairs, he would quickly group the tin soldiers into a squad and pretend to be drilling them when the door opened. And every night he would put them away in their box. All except the one-legged tin soldier. The little boy would always knock him over and leave him lying on the table. Did the tin soldier mind? Of course not! He could spend his nights gazing up at that dreamy face and gorgeous torso, gleaming in the glow of the night-light.

Then it happened. Was it the wicked golliwog or was

it the wind? Who can tell? But one morning, the little tin soldier flew out the window of the nursery and fell thirteen floors to the wide river that flowed past the little boy's building. *Plop!* He landed in an old sneaker that was floating past, and there he stood in it, for all the world like a marine standing guard over his ship.

The sneaker caught in a mess of lumber and plastic jugs and used condoms. The whole thing got stuck under a dark bridge. "To be sure," thought the tin soldier, "this is the evil golliwog's doing! Ah, but if only my G.I. Joe were in my ship sailing with me, I would not care if it were twice as dark and smelly!"

Just then a great rat crawled across the garbage. Seeing the tin soldier's face he mistook him for some animal he could eat and began gnawing on his shako. My, how it hurt! But the tin soldier kept his silence and gripped his bayonet still tighter. Now the frustrated rodent pulled the tin soldier from his vessel with his sharp jaws and threw him into the dark rushing waters. Down went the soldier through the depths and came to rest in the mouth of the body of a decomposing drug dealer, which was being dragged along the river bottom by the current. Could you imagine a more horrible fate for the brave little soldier? As the corpse bumped and rolled over rocks and old refrigerators, he found himself being jerked down by the motion into the gullet of the criminal, and thence into what was left of his stomach.

Never did the tin soldier move so much as an eyelash. He held himself erect, he clung to his bayonet, he kept his eyes forward, even though he was up to his shako in rotting viscera. Terrified though he was, for only fools are unafraid, he sustained himself with the thought of his beautiful infantryman, guardian of the nursery.

Now fish tore at the carcass of the drug peddler. Once

again the tin soldier was cast forth into the dark waters. He tumbled down through the murky depths, coming to rest on something soft and squishy. Then there was a creaking sound and a click. Every last flicker of light disappeared, and the little tin soldier lay in the silence of the grave.

For many months he lay thus, retaining his courage, shouldering his bayonet, eyes fixed firmly forward, resolute to the end. Then one day he felt his watery coffin being pulled upward, or so it seemed, and turned over and over, now at rest, now in motion, now being picked up once more.

Suddenly there was light! *"Dios!"* exclaimed a voice. It was a cook, and the soldier was lying in a large Chesapeake oyster, in the very kitchen of the little boy's parents' apartment! She seized the tin soldier between her finger and thumb and rushed to the nursery, where the little boy's father and mother sat beside the little boy's bed. And there still on the shelf, keeping watch over all below him, was the beautiful, brave, bronzed G.I. Joe, as handsome as ever, his helmet still thrust forward, his clear blue eyes still missing nothing, his powerful fists still gripping his mighty weapon.

Oh, how the little tin soldier's heart burst for joy to see him again! The G.I. Joe had been steadfast too. The tin soldier's eyes could have wept tin tears, but that would not have been proper. He looked at G.I. Joe, and G.I. Joe looked at him, and neither needed to say a word.

"Mira!" said the cook excitedly. "Is miracle, is miracle!"

"Get that thing out of here!" screamed the little boy's mother and threw the tin soldier into the roaring fire in the fireplace. For, as everyone knows, tin soldiers aren't really made of tin, but of lead. And her little boy had chronic lead poisoning.

So now the little tin soldier stood in the blazing flames. The heat he felt was terrible, but he could not tell whether it came from the fire or from the love in his faithful heart. He was aware, too, that he had been disgraced and punished, but he knew not for what. Still, even as he felt himself melting, he stood upright, shako firm, bayonet at the ready, resolute to the very, very end. His eyes were fixed on the G.I. Joe so far above him, and the G.I. Joe's were fixed on him.

Then suddenly—no one ever really found out why— the G.I. Joe toppled off the shelf into the fire. Even as the last piece of the tin soldier—his shako—melted, the G.I. Joe flared up brilliantly and was gone.

In the ashes the next day, the maid found a lump of lead in the shape of a heart, and clenched around it inseparably, a chunk of burned plastic shaped like a fist.

P.S. The little boy recovered, suffering some minor brain damage. He later entered West Point.

———

From *Poor Richard's Almanac of Modern Wisdom*:

All work and no play makes Jack VP Marketing for the entire East Coast.

Spider and the Stones

A FOLKTALE OF THE ATSINA

Nihaat the Spider was one of the most important deities of the Atsina, buffalo hunters and gatherers of the Northwest. Nihaat was a mischievous fellow who could perform extraordinary feats of magic and had ridiculous adventures as he ambled around.

Spider was restless. He could never sit still long. He was walking down the riverbank kicking a gourd when he saw Bear walking along the other bank and resolved to have some fun with him.

"Hey, Bear!" called Spider. "Have I ever told you how incredibly stupid you are? You're so dumb you don't know how to clean yourself after you defecate. I can see small turds hanging from the fur around your rectum right now, which look like salmonberries on the bushes in summer."

Although Spider only meant what he said as a joke or jesting game, Bear became very angry and splashed across the river to get at his tormentor. Spider, seeing that Bear had taken his words to heart, was frightened and ran away. Bear followed him, and by the look of rage on his face, Spider knew he meant business. He ran for higher ground, and soon he came upon a large pile of Stones in a narrow gully. He got an idea.

"Brothers," he said to the Stones, "build me a sturdy longhouse here!"

Nothing happened. Spider could see Bear was coming after him.

"Stones!" he shouted. "I command you to fly together, right now, into a strong secure longhouse so that I will be safe from Bear!"

Still nothing happened. Spider was getting scared and angry.

"Hey, Stones," he yelled. "You better do what I say. I'm an important deity of the Atsina, and you're supposed to cooperate with my magic!"

"Listen, arachnid," said the topmost Stone of the pile. "We don't feel like it. We couldn't care less if Bear pulls your legs off and eats you alive."

Now Spider was angrier than a thunderhead in the hot time of year. Bear was so close he could hear him panting. Spider summoned up all his magic powers from the wind and the grass and the earth and the sky and rolled them tight together and beat the pile of Stones with them to bend them to his will. Nothing.

"Give it up, guy," said the Stone. "We're through. You think you can just come round here and wave some magic wand and *boom!* there's a longhouse? Forget it! You know how much sheer effort it takes for a Stone to even roll a little by itself, let alone fly through the fucking air and form a fucking longhouse? A lot, that's how much. There's inertia to overcome, gravity, then we have to jiggle around until everything fits tight, so it doesn't fall in on your stupid, fucking head. It's a huge expense of energy."

"These are mundane matters," hissed Spider. "We animals live on a spiritual plane, in touch with deeper forces, the ropes that bind the tepee of the world together. And I'm telling you, if you don't fly together and form a goddamn longhouse right now, I won't be responsible for the consequences."

"Fuck you!" said the Stone. "Fuck your deeper forces! You're a bunch of lazy slobs. Expecting to get by

on that jerk-off magic shit. Nature at your command!
Fuck you. You know your problem? You don't like work.
You want a nice, strong, safe stone longhouse? Get off
your lazy, fucking hunter-gatherer ass and build one."

Spider was terrified. Bear was just a few yards away.
He had stopped and was looking around for signs of Spider. In seconds he'd find the little gully where Spider and
the Stones were. And then . . .

"Please, brother Stones," he sobbed. "Save me. Fly
into a barricade across the gully to give me time to get
away. Otherwise it's curtains for Spider."

"Frankly, Mr. In-Touch-with-Nature Deity," said another Stone, "we don't give a shit. We're sick and tired
of watching you creeps amble around, talking about the
dignity of nature and freedom, while you throw us at
some poor dumb bag of meat on legs or pull fruit off our
brother trees and sister bushes. You guys take, take, take.
But what do you put back in?"

The other Stones agreed. Spider was quivering with
fear now, desperately trying to get them to be quiet. Bear
was right at the mouth of the gully. Spider was trapped.

"You know how much actual land it takes to support
one of you so-called hunters and gatherers," asked yet
another Stone. "Thousands of acres for one family unit.
Properly managed, that land could support hundreds of
family units. But *noooo*. Land management's beneath the
noble animals!"

"We leave the land as we found it—pristine," sobbed
Spider.

"Yeah, right," said the top Stone. "Pristine. Entirely
free of stone longhouses."

"What you guys need," said the second Stone, "is a
little preindustrial infrastructure. Draw up plans. Develop agricultural management techniques so there's

some cultural consistency. Build up support systems, including a viable defense system, like, say, stone longhouses where you can take shelter from hostile entities."

"You realize," said the third Stone, "that there are people—oh, all right, animals—to the south of here who've done just that? They have whole cities, complex economies, all kinds of cultural artifacts. These are people with some sense of self-awareness. These are people who will leave their mark on nature and history. So, what's your excuse, creepo?"

"You are right, brother Stones," whimpered Spider. "As soon as I rejoin my fellow animals, I will develop plans for real social infrastructure and stop depending on shabby rhetorical devices to disguise our cultural bankruptcy. But right now, p-p-please give my magic just one tiny little last chance and fly together in some way to protect me!"

"Up yours," said the top Stone. "Hey, Bear! He's over here!"

So Bear pulled Spider's legs off and ate him all up.

Fuck You, Socrates

FROM PLATO'S *DISGORGIAS*

The great virtues of duty, love, obedience, etc., were bequeathed to Western civilization by the Greeks. And nowhere were they better learnt than under the great Greek teacher, Socrates.

(Callicles and Socrates are discussing the duties of the virtuous man.)

Callicles: May the virtuous man practice one virtue but ignore another?

Socrates: The virtuous man cannot choose which virtues he will practice. The virtues are like the limbs and organs of a body. When all are in harmony, the body is well, but if one should fail, it becomes sick.

Callicles: How, Socrates, may we know virtue? Is that knowledge innate in us?

Socrates: No, we may know virtue only by being taught. The virtues of the dutiful life, to wit, discipline, obedience, loyalty, perseverance, and so on, can be grasped only by wise men. Wise men then inculcate those virtues into the young and ignorant. Whence we may conclude that for the young, hard work is the virtue that precedes all others.

Callicles: Is hard work, then, the greatest of virtues?

Socrates: No, merely the first. Just as a man may live without a leg but not without a heart, love is the greatest virtue. Love is the lifeblood of the body of virtues, the sap which runs through all the others.

Callicles: Love, then, must be inculcated in the young?

Socrates: Yes, indeed.

Callicles: But can love be taught? Surely we are taught rather that love is reason perceiving beauty? Let us take your friend Lysias here. He is beautiful, is he not? And when your reason perceives this beauty, love is the result?

Socrates: This is true.

Callicles: So you, who are forty-one, have been educated in the highest of all virtues by Lysias, who is nine.

Socrates: Let me remind you, dear friend, that this academy was founded to further the enlightenment of all young people, through the technique of Socratean dialogues, a form I created, whose rules are fixed, amongst them the role of the interlocutor, in this instance you. It is the interlocutor's task to expound the point of view I wish to demolish and then retire gracefully, rather than to marshal stupid, irrelevant arguments in a pathetic attempt to score cheap points.

Callicles: It is your goal, then, to win all your dialogues? It pains you to contemplate even the possibility of tanking?

Socrates: Those are the rules. The rules I drummed into you by force of discipline.

Callicles: And those rules, as Lysias can surely attest, were by no means the only thing you drummed into me.

Socrates: Your meaning, dear Callicles, eludes me.

Callicles: Would that I—rather than just my meaning—had eluded you. Yet let us return to the matter of love and how it may be taught. For I am at a loss to understand how Lysias, whose reason is yet unformed, perceiving you, who are far from beautiful, is being taught love.

Socrates: Before addressing that question, dear ex-pupil, let me point out that, unlike you, I still have all my hair and that, as Pausanias remarked recently, I look not a day over thirty-seven.

Callicles: In the matter of hair, dear Socrates, you are as much my superior as you are in the girth of your belly—as Pausanias also recently remarked to me, in keeping with his custom of never saying to your face what he says to the rest of Athens.

Socrates: Pausanias is the illegitimate daughter of two mad dogs.

Callicles: Most rationally put, Socrates. And yet Pausanias once occupied that place in your affections now enjoyed by Lysias. As did I before him. Where is the love we were—supposedly—taught?

Socrates: Do not confuse affection with knowledge of

that higher form of love that exists between two souls. The day passes once the sun sets, yet have we the knowledge that the sun will rise again and another day come. Similarly, while affections pass, yet have we the knowledge that love will rise again, and come again.

Callicles: In every sense. And we Ancient Greeks have a word for this higher form of love, do we not?

Socrates: Before answering that, dear Callicles, let me say how happy I am that you have renounced your former impudence and are now participating in Socratean dialogue according to its most important rule, namely, that you ask questions to which you already know the answer in order that Socrates may ultimately triumph. Yes, we Ancient Greeks do have a word for it, many words in fact. *Eros, eran, philia, agape, aphrodisia.*

Callicles: Eros, is it not, is that love that exists between an *erastes* and his *eromenos?* You are the erastes, Lysias the eromenos? Though Lysias as the junior partner in this love may also be called the *pais* or *paidika?* Hence you, as the erastes of Lysias the paidika, may also be known as a *paiderastes?*

Socrates: Proudly so. Though elegiac poets might prefer to call me *paidophiles* since it scans better.

Callicles: And we Ancient Greeks hold the love of a pederast, or pedophile, for his eromenos as the highest form of love we know?

Socrates: Indeed, for we Ancient Greeks also hold that women lack the moral insight and firmness of purpose to resist the temptations of comfort and pleasure as men can; we segregate them because of their shameless enjoyment of sexual intercourse and their natural inclination to adultery.

Callicles: Granted, but is not this highest form of eros, that of the pederast for his eromenos, a bag with but one opening, a road down which only one may travel? So I ask again, how is love taught to young Lysias here? For when I occupied the same place in your affections he now enjoys, I learnt only that love was something running down my leg.

Socrates: Once again I see my victory in this dialogue growing more distant.

Callicles: Forgive my boldness, dear Socrates. One last question and you may triumph.

Socrates: Dear Callicles, the boldness of your mind may always be forgiven—particularly since it is attached to so handsome a pair of thighs. Ask on.

Callicles: Let us predicate that the love, or eros, of a paiderastes for his eromenos, which we find to be the highest of virtues, became in another place or time repugnant. Let us suppose that some misguided future non-Greeks saw the practice—as I was stupid enough to do—from the side of the eromenos rather than—as is correct—from the side of the paiderastes. What if, to put it bluntly, these foolish mortals held the intercrural and anal screwing of young boys to be no virtue whatsoever?

Socrates: Observe self-discipline, Callicles, and temper your language. Young ears are present.

Callicles: My deepest apologies, dear master, and to you, Lysias. This, however, is the crux of my question. Since love is the greatest of the virtues, and since eros between pederast and eromenos is a supreme expression of it, would not these misguided future non-Greeks be correct in rejecting all our virtues? For, as you have convincingly shown, love is the lifeblood of all other virtues.

Socrates: Your logic is faultless, dear friend; only your supposition is absurd. Finally I scent my well-earnt victory! In theory such men would be correct in rejecting all the virtues we embrace if they found so central a virtue as love between paiderastes and eromenos repugnant. The virtue of courage we Ancient Greeks espouse, for example, cannot exist without love between warriors. For example, that between Achilles and his eromenos Patroklos. And the fire of all other virtues, such as obedience, perseverance, loyalty, discipline, cannot burn without the fuel of love between pupil and master. Were a man in some future age to hold up these virtues for the young to imitate, yet at the same time reject the love that, as it were, makes them stick, that man would be either an idiot or a charlatan. But your hypothesis, while amusing, is impossible. The wisdom of the ancients, the admonition of the gods, the example of Zeus' love for Ganymede, and the evidence of our own reason shows conclusively that eros between paiderastes and eromenos is a supreme virtue.

Callicles: I acknowledge, in the most heartfelt manner, your victory, dear friend. However, in the matter of eros, my rectum rebuts your dictum.

Socrates: Latin! I have warned you before, old friend, against this obscene usage of a language that does not yet exist. Never darken my doors again.

Callicles: We Ancient Greeks have one more word for it, Socrates. And the word is this: Fuck you.

V

SELF-INDULGENCE

cigarettes, or all of the above. In the old countries pleasure and privilege went hand in hand; hence the underprivileged who make up the melting pot have always seen limitless Fun as an expression of their freedom. Hedonism is as American as applejack, heart attacks, and hot fudge sundaes.

Simultaneously, at the other end of steerage, almost as many millions followed in the footsteps of the Puritans, seeing America as a moral tabula rasa where a bright, shiny, spanking-new Eden could be set up, free of the filth and grime and hospital corners of sin. For these folks, too, the pleasures of the flesh were associated with old-country corruption and privilege, but they were fleeing them, not looking for them. The expression of their freedom was a limitless *lack* of Fun. As a result, America has always had more prudes per square foot than any country outside of fundamentalist Islam. The peculiarity of American prudes is that they regard Eden as more than a state of mind or a distant prospect of heavenly reward; it's a place right here and now and it must be kept clean. That means you, Buster Brown. Thus only in America could citizens amend their Constitution to impose Prohibition. Only in America would citizens organize to kill other citizens in freshly laundered sheets.

In the never-ending tug-of-war between hedonism and Edenism, self-indulgence has the advantage of being as old as the hills. It seems unlikely that humans will ever overcome their need to get drunk, laid, stoned, wasted, too full, or, simply, off. On the other hand, in a country where the belief that history is bunk is widely held, being as old as the hills is not always an acceptable defense. Edenism thrives these days, not just among the white-robed saints of the right, but on the worried, caring, sharing faces of the post-socialist left. Disapproval of pleasure drips from the stalactites of the Christian Coalition, to form stalagmites of nutritional, behavioral, and sexual correctness. Nineties neo-Puritans take as their inspiration AA, not the KKK. They're quite capable of removing A. E. Housman from the school library on the grounds that he wrote:

> And malt does more than Milton can
> To justify God's ways to man.

But then they don't like Milton—a Puritan—either. Too Eurocentric. Too corrupt. Too privileged. Too old country.

Here's a curious thing about lefty pleasure-virgins. While the troglodyte right believes that Christ will reward its self-denial (and its persecution of the self-indulgent) with eternal bliss, the pleasure-virgins have no such prospect. No God, no Heaven, no Hell. Just seventy-odd years of pure, clean living and then—lights out. Which raises an intriguing question: For whom or what are they saving themselves?

Don't make that mistake. Wallow in self-indulgence. Ignore the warning label. Rip it open, lick it, kiss it, fondle it, rub it on your cheek, crush it to your lips, let it run down your chin, tear great juicy hunks of it from the bone with slippery fingers, sip it, gulp it, suck it, swallow it, slather it on your skin, rub it on your nipples, stroke it till it moans, sit in it, lie in it, wriggle around in it so it fills every nook and cranny in your body. Do it often. Do it hard.

The Twelve Steps to Guiltless Pleasure

This useful little meditation was developed by the members of Guiltaholics Anonymous.

1. We admitted the power of alcohol, that it made our lives more manageable.
2. Came to believe that a Power greater than ourselves had provided the means, one day at a time, to restore our sanity.
3. Made a decision to thank God, whoever He or She might be, for decreeing that while the arrow of life is decay, decay would provide the means to keep decay at bay.
4. Made a searching moral inventory of what God might possibly find wrong in billions of humans over thousands of years finding some small solace from the vicissitudes of life and the hardship of their labor in a glass or two of fermented fruit.
5. Admitted to God, to ourselves, and to the bartender the exact nature of our order.
6. Were entirely ready to have God remove all those defective characters who, having been unable to control pleasure in their own lives, now sought to control it in the lives of others.
7. Humbly asked God to remove the enemies of pleasure from our face, our glass, and our plate.
8. Made a list of all the persons harmed down through the years by people who considered themselves morally cleansed, and then gave up because it was far too long.

9. Made direct amends to such persons, wherever possible, by sharing with them the best available bottle of God's greatest earthly gift, except where to do so would injure them or others.

10. Continued to take inventory of the benefits bestowed by alcohol on the arts, cultures, economies, and religions of the world's greatest civilizations, and gave that up too because the list was even longer than the one in Step 8.

11. Sought through prayer and meditation to improve contact with the Power that forces the juice through the vine and forms the bubbles in the yeast, seeking to know His or Her will for us in deciding what might go with the grilled salmon.

12. Having had a spiritual awakening as a result of these steps, we vowed to carry this message to alcohol lovers everywhere, shamed and intimidated by prigs, prudes, busybodies, and scaremongers, and to practice these principles in all our affairs, especially at lunch. Then, with a lighter, healthier heart, we went home to a good night's sleep.

From the Rolls-Royce Owner's Manual

Remember: However bad things get, every Silver Cloud has a lining.

The Lovesong of J. Alfred Dahmer

AFTER T. S. ELIOT

Let us go then, you and I
When the evening is spread out against the sky
Like a person mesmerized upon a table
Ready to eat.
Let us go through certain half-deserted streets
Promising each other treats
And restless bites in one-night cheap hotels
(Say, did you hear the dinner bell?)
And meat that's full of tedious ligaments.
My insidious intent,
To lead you to that all-important question. . . .
No, do not ask "What is it?"
First, come and pay a visit.

The Last Gourmet

It's 2045. Utopia has arrived. Be warned.

The voices came from so far away.

"What *is* this dump? It's geeksome."

Women, youngish. Sixty-five, seventy tops. Could've had a voice job though.

"Years ago used to be called Bistro Mistral. Slobs came up here to indulge. Jugs, meat, fish, fossil fuels, tobacco, you name it."

Guy. Older. Official twang. Maybe Nice Police. Got to get out. Bury quail bones. Why so dark?

Aha. Eyes closed. Time to open eyes. Shit, damn, and Shirley. They are cops, and they ain't in the next room. Dead to rights. Curse that '97 Dows!

He was strapped to a body-form Mort-Port. There was a pillow under his head, a sheet discreetly up to his nose. Soooo nice the Nice Police, soooo caring. They thought he might be dead, but they weren't absolutely sure, and they'd tried to make him comfortable. And who could blame them? These days people vacationed in the afterlife. You never knew if someone had bought the farm or was just renting.

The motherly hum of an electric chopper flattened the redwood saplings outside. Probably CalMed. Whoever it was, it was all over now, Baby Blue. They'd find the cellar, put two and two together, vaporize the place. *Adieu la vie.*

Last night he'd sat where he used to, so long ago. His favorite table in the corner overlooking the ocean. No table these days, no corner. Just an old door on some rocks and a rotten skeleton of studs. But the Pacific still heaved in the starlight. The burnt, thyme-y succulence of the little birds still gave him goose bumps. And that old Ridge Montebello Cab was like drinking Mother Earth.

"He's alive." The medic. A real boy, this one, not a day over forty-five.

"He's not OOB, either."

Stupid little owl kisser. Why would he be OOB? Unlike every other occupant of the great nation-state, he liked being in his body.

He felt the warm embrace of the gen-scan on his testicles. Soon the kid would be reading off the tiny screens implanted in his retinae. His whole life flashing before someone else's eyes.

The stats rattled off: name, aliases, transplants, real age . . .

"Can you believe this boom's only ninety-five years old? Some people just won't take care of themselves."

Here it comes.

"Holy Bill Wilson! This character's got a record yay long. 1996, five to ten for DWI . . ."

"DWI?" The rookie was puzzled.

"Directing while impaired. He used to be in NET. Non-electronic Teledrama. Served seven years. Back inside in 2010 for aggravated porcicide. Paroled 2015. 2020 to 2030 in and out of rehab, jug-smuggling, suspected anti-Vegan, cattle raising. This slob's done it all."

"Why's he up here in the woods? To die? He oughta be in a MedArcade."

"He ain't dying." The older cop's voice was hard. He'd guessed. Shit. "Read his contents."

A warm probe passed round the top of his pants. The runty medic hopped with excitement.

"INCREDIBLE! This geeko has MEAT in his tubes. I can't read it exactly, but it looks like . . . BIRD!"

The rookie retched. "How could anyone . . ." She burst into tears. "Those sweet fluffy little . . ."

Ah, shaddup, you little cucumber-humper.

One eyelid was forced up. The hand-laser bore into his eye. The medic stood up half-laughing with disbelief.

"WOWOO! Alcohol! I only saw this in med school. He must have five, six hundred cc's of wine in him!"

That was it. The meat set off the gals; the booze set off the guys.

The big Nicer grabbed him by his shirt and yanked him up, still strapped to the Mort-Port. He was an inch

from the cop's clean-smelling face. No garlic, no lar-
doons, no béchamel had ever passed this lawman's lips.

"A gourmet, huh? Listen, geeko. If it wasn't for the
fact that I love you deeply as a fellow traveler and really
want to share your predicament . . . I'd smash your
brains in with a rock."

The cop threw him back to the ground with a bone-
crunching crash.

"Book him."

*   *   *

Whatever drug they'd given him wore off abruptly. He
felt terrific. Okay. Got it, back in mini-court, strapped to
a Narca-Lounger. On the screen two women and a man
in their low hundreds. Fit, tanned, nice-looking people.
Judge and jury rolled into one. Speedy trial, California
style.

They were in the middle of something.

"Patrick, of all these charges, first-degree avicide is
by far the most serious . . ."

Avicide. Ah, yes. That would be the quail.

"You face two consecutive twenty-five-year terms for
that alone."

So he'd been found guilty while he was asleep. That
was the nice thing about J-'n'-Js. No messy testimony,
no messy cross-examination.

"But we'd like to propose something to you."

Plea-bargain? Turn in the others? There were no others. Palates gone the way of palaces. Carnivores the way
of cars. Alison, Bryan, Joshua, Daniel . . .

"Your lifetime utility-futility spectrum is one of a
kind, Pat."

The man was speaking now.

"We're talking deep violet, old buddy. I don't get it.

Killing the feathered to consume their bodies isn't just murder and cannibalism. It's suicide. That stuff kills you, pally. Ditto wine. Poison, Pat. We do all we can to help—eradicate airborne yeasts, the works. It's over, Pat. Choose life.''

The guy was right. It was over. Once you could smuggle it, but no longer. An image floated through his mind—a magnum of Château Gloria roped to the transmission of a Mexican pickup. Sweet days gone by. Then they stamped out yeasts from one end of the continent to the other. Like smallpox. Now there was no one to buy from. Just caches here and there everyone had forgotten. The Bistro's cellar. They'd have wiped it out by now. Ancient clarets, stately zins, sauternes the color of Rembrandt's light, autumnal ports and Madeiras, carted off to a mile-deep toxic dump. Bottles recycled into solar panels. Perhaps it *was* time to check out.

The woman was speaking now.

"What we're trying to evaluate is whether we're at fault. For trying to block this drive of yours toward self-destruction. Perhaps we should flow with the river of your life . . .''

The other woman now. Nice tits for a centenarian.

"We wonder if you're searching for a way to communicate something to us that you can only express through actions . . .''

What the fuck . . . ? Images were suddenly thickening in his mind. A soft terrine of wild rabbit and cepes he'd had somewhere called La Mignonette in Paris in the 1980s. He'd just discovered gewürztraminer. He could feel the spicy bitterness of it against the fat of the terrine . . . Coquillages took over, spilling themselves into the mouth of his . . . What was happening?

The man again. He seemed more distant, as if the

camera had pulled back. But the screen was smaller too. Was the Narca-Lounger rolling somewhere?

". . . Take a long vacation on the other side. Perhaps settle down there. Know what I mean?"

Yeah, he knew. The bastards! He had to fight. But the images took over again, realer than before. Now they were from underground times, stolen and smuggled fruits, the sweeter for being prohibited. A trout by the river sizzling in dirty butter. Oh, the savor! Sirens coming nearer. Gotta get back! Gotta get up!

"I . . . have . . . right . . . choose . . ."

"Of course you do, Pat," said the first woman sweetly. "All prisoners choose their own restitutional method. We wouldn't impose anything on you without a clear signal . . ."

OOBers swore the afterlife was alc-free and veg. Someone claimed to have met Christ, who said it wasn't wine at the Last Supper but a soft drink made from dates . . . He was slipping. Effort! NOW!

"I . . . choose . . . life. . . . Deuteronomy 30.19."

All three smiled at him. Gently, lovingly, sadly.

Chief Joseph Speaks Once More

Chief Joseph's moving "Letter to His Father in Washington" was probably written by a well-intentioned Anglo-Saxon who got all squishy inside every time he or she thought about noble savages. Chief Joseph's great-great-great grandson has a slightly different take on the matter.

The president in Washington sends word that he wishes to give us back our land. But how can we buy or sell the sky? The idea is strange to us. Even if we own the freshness of the air and the sparkle of the water, how can we sell them? Every part of this earth is sacred to my people. But what kind of money can we make off shining pine needles, sandy shores, mist in the dark woods, meadows, humming insects? The shining water that moves in the streams has to be not just water but our lifeblood.

If you give us back our land, you must remember it is sacred. The water's murmur is the voice of the blackjack dealer. It quenches our thirst; it feeds our children. So you must give this silver river the kindness you would give your father and forget about slapping any taxes on it.

If you give us back our land, remember that air is precious to us and that what we breathe into it is sacred also. The weed that gave our grandfather his first breath also receives his last sigh. So if you give us back our land, we will keep it apart and sacred as a place where man can come to taste the weed that is sweetened by the great tobacco flowers. And forget about taxing that as well.

Your destiny is a mystery to us. What will happen when the plains are once more full of buffalo and wild horses and swift ponies? What will happen when the secret corners of the forest are free of men and talking wires and iron beasts? What will happen when the land is covered with thickets and the sky is dark with eagles? What will happen when the air is pure and sweet and the weed is banished utterly from it? How will you survive? Where on this sacred earth will fun-loving guys and gals go to live a little?

So if you give us back our land, remember this: You will love it here. Here in our land you will hear the soft hum of the wheels, the sweet whisper of rustling cards, the gentle chirping of the dice. Hold in your mind a land where all is green—the velvety turf of the tables, the eye-shades of the dealers, the tree on which money grows.

Here your grandfather's eyes will see acres of fruit, cherries, plums, oranges, and lemons; his gnarled hands will scoop silver from a waterfall of coins. Here in our land, soothing rivers of whiskey flow, here gentle mists of blue smoke swirl, here night and time are unknown. We will preserve it for you—and your children—so come on down, God love ya!

The Tortoise and the Hare

FROM TALES BY ASSOP

This delightful tale teaches us almost nothing other than the pointlessness of organized sports.

A hare—which many people confuse with rabbits but are actually related to the deer family—once met a tortoise.

"Gee, you're slow!" said the hare. "Old creepy, that's what you are. I'd like to see you in the thousand meters; it'd be a joke!"

And so on and so forth went the hare, for hares tend to be harebrained and talk too much. Eventually the tortoise got a word in edgewise.

"Old creepy, huh?" said the tortoise slowly. "Let's race, and we'll see who wins, hareface."

"You're on, you're on!" said the hare excitedly. "Who'll be our starter?"

"Hm, let's think. How about the fox?" suggested the tortoise—though it took ages for him to say it.

"Okay, okay, okay," said the hare and fetched the fox.

The fox was quite up on animal races, and he suggested that they use the shoulder of a deserted piece of highway, so that it would be easy on the tortoise. He marked out one thousand meters, helped the tortoise to the starting line, got the hare to sit still long enough to line up also, and . . .

They were off!

The hare shot ahead. The fox, knowing that the hare would probably take a nap somewhere along the course and that the slow but steady tortoise was more likely to win, set off in a leisurely manner for the finish line.

Imagine his surprise when he rounded the curve and there was the hare, toweling off by the finish line, scarcely winded. The fox's helper—a hedgehog— scurried up carrying a big stopwatch.

"Amazing time!" said the hedgehog. "Forty-four point eight seconds. Could be a record for this neck of the woods. Perhaps even for the county."

"Wow!" said the fox, looking admiringly at the hare. "We're going to have to work a little with you. Perhaps get you into the All-State Small-Mammal Trials."

"Great!" replied the hare.

"Know something?" said the fox. "You're really very attractive." (I forgot to say that the hare was a girl.)

"Well, thanks, big fella," said the hare, smiling in a pretty inviting way. "You're no slouch yourself."

"Women athletes!" The fox smiled back. "When you guys get all sweated from a race, man, it drives me crazy!"

So they found an abandoned badger's sett just off the highway and went at it. Talk about the beast with two backs! They must've done the dirty at least two dozen times, every which way from Sunday. Neither the fox nor the hare had ever had sex that fabulous with anyone.

And the tortoise? Well, it took her (did I forget to say the tortoise was a girl too?) the rest of the day and evening to get about seventy meters down the course. Finally—exhausted—she fell asleep, right there on the shoulder. The fox found her the next day, just after she woke up, weeping quiet little tortoise tears over her defeat. Being a softhearted fellow and—frankly—feeling pretty much full of the milk of human kindness after the night's activities, the fox decided to organize some special games just for tortoises. Everyone in the forest pitched in, and the Speed-Challenged Olympics were held the next day, with all the events being things that would actually empower tortoises like Synchronized Swimming, Shell-Schussing, and Imitating a Rock.

The whole thing was a stunning success, and everyone lived happily ever after—at least until the next forest fire.

The Great Wives of France

BY ALEXIS LE CHIN

> The French, as the old saying goes, are a funny race. They fight with their feet and make love with their face.

God created wife to make glad the heart of man, sang the psalmist, and of all the wives of the world, few taste more sublime than those of France.

Dégustation de femmes is a millennial tradition, which the French have refined over countless years into an art; French wives, as a result, have been in demand all over the world for centuries. After the First World War, demand so far outstripped supply that unscrupulous merchants began exporting wives of inferior quality with time-honored French names to unsuspecting—and in some cases woefully ignorant—foreign consumers. Many of these wives came, not from France, but from Spain, Italy, or even Algeria, exhibiting a coarseness and lack of style that seriously undermined the reputation of French wives as a whole. (This is not to criticize Italian and Spanish wives, which have their own charms, although those of Algeria are uniformly an insult to the most courageous venophile's palate.)

In the 1930s, therefore, an enlightened government program was instituted strictly regulating which wives could and could not describe themselves as French. The two chief categories are: 1. Wives raised and matured under strict supervision in a given area. These carry the designation *Appellation d'Orifice Contrôlée*. This applies to some thirty-five percent of all French wives. 2. Wives of lesser quality, raised and matured under less stringent laws, which are classed as *Femmes Délimités de Qualité Supérieure*. This designation applies to some five percent of the whole. All other wives, while many may be full-bodied and of excellent bouquet, flavor, etc., are considered *femmes de consommation* or *femmes ordinaires*. It is this type of wife that is downed by millions of Frenchmen every night.

As global competition has increased in the latter part of the twentieth century, particularly from California, French producers have developed other nontraditional categories. It would once have been unthinkable for the French to offer California-style "jug-wives," but many producers now do just that; more legitimate are the generic styles of wife known as "marietals," or, in industry parlance, "fighting marietals." Quite unacceptable is the growing practice of exporting very young wives, long before they are ready, many of them far below the age of scent.

The question of how well French wives travel is an age-old one, but to my mind very much a red herring. Many fine French wives react badly to too much handling—they tend to become harsh and bitter. But the same criticism used to be leveled at California wives, particularly the whites. We now know that traveling actually improves them; long-distance driving in high temperatures on leather upholstery imparts to California wives their characteristic tang. Similarly, long hours spent in the confined quarters of a modern jet deepen the elusive, savory earthiness for which classic French wives have always been prized.

The importance of tanning is also hotly debated. Tanning, of course, is a by-product of the skin, but how much tanning a wife needs is an open question. Too much tanning (e.g., one hundred percent) will impart a hard leathery flavor. Too little will make the wife pale and unappetizing. The robust red and pink wives of southern France, for instance, always benefit from generous amounts of tanning. In this area also Californians have mounted a challenge. They believe that huge amounts of tanning allow their wives to maintain quality as they age (or, as they put it, it gives the wife "legs"). Even Californian blush wives have far more tanning than their French counterparts.

The growing and maturing process need not overly concern the aspiring venophile. Old-fashioned methods have long given ground to scientific ones. In the old days a wife was seeded in the early spring and would be up the next morning. But it was a hit-and-miss matter, with no guarantee of quality, involving traditional wooden tools and utensils. The necessity of corking and uncorking, over and over again, for mandatory daily tastings, was laborious; it was a constant and arduous struggle to protect a wife from foreign bodies.

Nowadays the science of venology has revolutionized the ancient craft of wife-husbandry. Malolactation is common, as is the judicious use of various chemicals. I view with approval, however, the current trend away from chemicals and back to natural techniques; in particular, I have always abominated the use of sprays. One traditional custom has recently reappeared: that of maturing French wives indoors. (Californian and Australian wives, by contrast, are brought to maturity outdoors, often in woods.)

And so to the actual tasting. Tasting is a delicate but rewarding process, and the wife lover will benefit enormously by following a few simple guidelines, as laid down by the Société Internationale des Grands Maîtres de Tastefemme.

First, no wife should be chilled. Cool, yes; chilled, no. The rule of thumb is that white wives should be enjoyed at slightly less than room temperature; contrary to common belief, this is true also of more robust ruby-tinted wives, who tend to heat up of their own accord.

The wife should be opened about half an hour prior to tasting to give her time to breathe; if she begins to breathe too fast, some chilling is appropriate.

Tasting proceeds as follows. Place the opened wife on the table. Bring the nose to within an inch or so of the surface of the wife and inhale deeply to savor the full bouquet, or "nose." For many experts—especially in blind tastings—this will tell them all they need to know about age, place of origin, degree of tanning, etc. And for many—myself included—it is frequently the supreme pleasure, be it the sea-breeze savor of a Blonde de

Blondes matured *sur lit* or the deep, dark, trufflelike scents of a venerable Margot.

Step two: Take a generous mouthful of the wife and roll it round and round the mouth with the tongue. Here the taster looks for balance, the perfect combination of skin, juice, body, and acidity. Without question, this is the most delicious part of the experience and one where the taster abandons himself or herself utterly to the flavor of the wife, a process that can take anywhere from twenty seconds to a long weekend.

Finally, the taster gently expels the mouthful and replaces the wife back on the table. Now is the time to savor the aftertaste, or "finish." A long finish is a point of honor with the French, for it is the mark of a great wife. To qualify in this category, the finish should still be detectable after several minutes. Once again, however, it should be said that the taste of some truly world-class French wives (e.g., a vintage Mum) can linger for weeks.

One final footnote for the fledgling *tastefemme*. At no point, and under no circumstances, should any attempt be made to swallow a wife.

VI

EGOTISM

Looking out for Number One and being Number One are not the same thing. While it's true that those who are Number One have got that way by looking out for Number One to the exclusion of all else, looking out for Number One does not guarantee that you will *be* Number One. But it will make you happy.

Hardly surprising. Who, after all, is more important than Number One? Hundreds of millions of people will go to bed hungry tonight, but however much sympathy you feel for them, not a single one of those experiences of starvation is one iota as important as your inhaling a nice juicy cheeseburger. Hundreds of millions of people have died in this century, many in hideously painful circumstances, but not one of those deaths, however much it cried out to humanity, is of the slightest importance compared to the reality that you, someday, must croak.

Sympathy is, after all, just pumped-up good manners. When push comes to shove, there's only one person who can have your experiences, and that's you. Look out for them, guard them, treasure them. They're all you've got. Even Mother Teresa, as she lifts the ravaged skeleton of a starving leper onto the gurney—remembering to pick his nose up from the dirt where it fell and place it gently at his side—is doing all this only because it makes her in some profound way feel good. If she didn't do it, she wouldn't feel good. She's looking out for Number One.

Looking out for Number One can be the very opposite of trying to be Number One. We live in a society preoccupied with winning. Whether we're being exhorted to do our duty or being urged to bend the rules, the assumed reward is that we will Win. Never mentioned in the ideology of winning, however, is the simple fact that even the smallest of competitions (two people) must have at least one loser. Most competitions involve many people. They all have one winner and many losers. Defining society as a series of competitions to be won, in other words, guarantees that it will be a society made up, overwhelmingly, of losers.

Don't listen to those who tell you to strive, to do your duty, or even to bend the rules and win at all costs. They only want to keep you busy being a loser so they can get theirs. They're looking out for Number One.

The Marriage of Art and Commerce

Once upon a time, for reasons which need not concern us, Ernest Hemingway and Samuel Goldwyn got lost in the desert. It was a burning hot morning and since neither had bothered to bring anything to drink, they were soon desperately thirsty. Noon came and went without a glimmer of water or a vestige of civilization; by early afternoon they were seeing mirages and were reduced to crawling on their hands and knees. Then, as the merciless sun began to dip toward the horizon, Hemingway spotted a tiny puddle of water in the shade of a rocky outcrop—scarcely more than a few mouthfuls, but enough to keep them alive.

He made for the puddle on all fours, but Goldwyn outstripped him. The legendary author was sure the legendary producer meant to steal all the water for himself. When he got to the puddle, however, Goldwyn stood up groggily and after fumbling for a while with his pants, took a long piss in it.

"What the fuck are you doing?" screamed Hemingway.

"What the fuck do you think I'm doing, asshole?" Goldwyn yelled back. "I'm making it better!"

If

Let's say that you're a most ambitious stripling
Who while the sun shines *wants* to make some hay;
If you your values learn from Rudyard Kipling,
You need your head examined right away.

If you can keep your job when all your cronies
Are losing theirs and blaming it on you,
If you can vote yourself a massive bonus,
Despite the quarter's plunging revenue;
If you can wait and not be tired by waiting
To sink the knife exactly where it fits,
And being hated beat them all at hating,
And then downsize them all, the stupid shits;

If you can dream of sex all through a meeting
With hot account execs from O & M,
But never give a hint, however fleeting,
Your mind's on anything but cpm's;
If you can slap and tickle without feeling,
Give new meaning to the phrase "a bottom line";
If you can reinforce that glassy ceiling
(And fire the silly ninnies when they whine);

If you can stop a whistleblower blowing
And make sure the bastard never works again;
If you can inside trade without it showing
And when the feds call, neatly shift the blame;
If you can peddle stuff that causes cancer
But know the art of making settlements;

If you can perjure smoothly when you answer
And have the court seal all your documents;

If you can sell your board stupendous hooey;
If you can sweet-talk *Fortune* magazine;
If you can screw—but never be the screwee;
If you can count the all-important bean;
If you can fill each ever-loving minute
With sixty seconds of concern for Number One,
The company is yours and all that's in it,
And—yes—you'll be the CEO, my son!

From *Poor Richard's Almanac of Modern Wisdom:*

In the country of the blind, the one-eyed man is pilot.

Rabbit Reflux

AFTER DOLT WISNEY

The animal-rights movement, not to mention certain vegetarians, take as gospel the idea that animals, left to themselves, would live harmoniously in a peaceable kingdom. In fact, every species on the planet exists by eating other species, as this action-packed little fable demonstrates.

Thumper ran excitedly to the foot of the old oak tree.
    "Wake up! Wake up!" he cried at the great hole in the cleft of the trunk.

For the moment nothing happened. Then Wise Old Mr. Owl appeared, rubbing his big round eyes. It was dawn, after all, and he'd just gotten to sleep after a hard night's hunting.

"Wha—?" he mumbled, blearily. "What now?"

"It's happened!" yelled Thumper. "A new Prince is born!"

"Well, well!" exclaimed Wise Old Mr. Owl, gradually coming awake. He coughed up a pellet of feathers, hair, and bone from the previous evening's supper and spat it on the ground. "This is quite an occasion!"

"It sure is, Mr. Owl," said Thumper. "Come quick!"

All of Thumper's brothers and sisters agreed. Wise Old Mr. Owl flew down beside Thumper.

"Yes, sir!" said the venerable bird.

"*AAAAAARGH,*" screamed Thumper as Wise Old Mr. Owl sank his sharp curved claws into Thumper's neck. All the other baby rabbits ran away.

"It's not every day a new Prince is born," said Wise Old Mr. Owl, tearing at Thumper's big cute left eye with his feather-covered bill. He broke through the hard outer skin of the eyeball and, getting a good grip on the retina, ripped the eye from its socket. Blood and retinal fluid spurted everywhere. Owl swallowed the whole thing.

"What's he called?" asked Wise Old Mr. Owl, starting on Thumper's big cute right eye.

"*NAAAH!* Not my eyes!!" pleaded Thumper, twisting in agony, trying desperately to get free from Wise Old Mr. Owl's claws. "Bambi! Sweet God of Rabbits, how that hurts!"

"Well," said Wise Old Mr. Owl, swallowing the second eyeball and turning his attention to Thumper's soft, vulnerable stomach, "Bambi's mom—the Queen of the Forest—is to be congratulated!"

feet. They were red and blue and black with cold. In her tattered apron she carried bundles of matches, and she held one in her hand—just in case a customer should come along. For she was a little match girl; that was her humble occupation. Few people bought her matches on the best of days, but sometimes a grand gentleman would need a match in a hurry to light his cigar or burn an important document. On New Year's Eve, however, the streets were empty. Everyone was at home, sitting down to a holiday dinner of roast goose. She could smell the delicious savory scents wafting from gaily lit windows as she limped through the snow. No one sought matches tonight. Cigars were already lit, important documents were forgotten. Every house blazed with candles. No one needed one of her sad little bundles on a night like this.

The snowflakes fell on her flaxen hair, there to become icy drops that dripped down her slender throat and trickled under her tattered bodice. But she thought not of her beauty. All she could think of was the cold. She drew her threadbare shawl closer around her thin shoulders. Up ahead was the magnificent portico of a splendid hotel. Perhaps if she huddled near its entrance she might be able to sell a bundle of matches and go home with a penny or two. She dared not go home without something, for if she did, her father would beat her again. Besides, it was freezing at home too. The packing crate she and her father and her brothers and sisters lived in had only a straw roof, full of holes. They stuffed rags from the garbage dump where they could, but beggars would steal the rags in the night to wrap around their feet, and then the bitter wind would whistle again through the holes.

She found a spot where the resplendently dressed doormen could not see her—just beyond the bright arc of light cast by the blazing gas lamps at the hotel's entrance. She sank exhausted on the pavement beside one of the mighty pillars that adorned the hotel's facade, drawing her delicate little feet under her skirts. Oh, how cold it was upon the ground! Even colder than when she stumbled through the drifts!

"Excuse me," said a voice from the darkness, "but this is my territory."

Wiping the snowflakes from her eyes, the little match girl peered round the pillar. There on the other side, hardly visible in the darkness and the swirling blizzard, sat—another little match girl! She, too, had a threadbare shawl drawn tightly around her thin shoulders and her bare feet, red and blue with cold, were drawn up under her tattered skirts in a desperate attempt to keep them warm. She, too, had flaxen hair and a slender throat and clutched in her apron sad little bundles of matches. The first little match girl felt so sorry for her that her heart almost burst with pity.

"There won't be enough activity tonight for two, I'm afraid," said the second little match girl, "so perhaps you'd better move on."

The first little match girl knew she was right. On a freezing New Year's Eve, they'd be lucky if even one grand person went in or out of the hotel, and even luckier if that person needed some matches. Only one little match girl could hope to make the paltry sum that was her due. And the other little match girl had been there first.

With despair in her heart, but conscious that she was doing the right thing, the first little match girl staggered to her feet.

"Thank you for being cooperative!" cried the other little match girl. "I did so want to avoid more stringent measures!"

The first little match girl turned despondently away into the night. Just then an enormous horseless brougham, its brass lanterns ablaze, drew up at the entrance to the hotel. A uniformed chauffeur sprang from the driving seat and leapt to open the rear door. From it emerged a rubicund old gentleman, bundled up in a wide hat of sable fur and an ankle-length sable coat. The head doorman sprang forward with a huge umbrella to keep the snowflakes from his hat; another, lesser, doorman sprang forward with a length of carpet to keep his soft leather shoes off the slush.

"Good heavens!" said the second little match girl. "It's Otto Kruger, the Swedish Match King!"

So saying, she jumped up and stumbled through the snow to the hotel entrance. The doormen, intent on their charge, did not notice her for a moment. She had just enough time to reach for the old gentleman's sleeve.

"Mr. Kruger! Mr. Kruger!" the second little match girl exclaimed with great excitement in her voice. "What a thrill this is! I am such an admirer of yours! Happy New Year!"

Hearing her words, the old gentleman paused. The chief doorman tried to loose her grip on his sleeve, but he waved the flunky away.

"Thank you, my dear," he boomed. "And a happy New Year to you too."

"See, Mr. Kruger," the second little match girl went on, holding up her bundles, "this is how much I believe in you and what you've done for the international match market. Even on this bitter night I'm out here in the snow, selling your product!"

Again the doormen tried to hustle her away, but now the Match King dismissed them imperiously and put a huge fur-clad arm around her slim form. As he gazed down at the second little match girl, his eyes brimmed with tears.

"My dear," he murmured with a catch in his voice, "I am touched beyond words. Were it not for countless loyal and unsung persons like yourself at the retail level, I would be a king without a kingdom."

"Oh, thank you, thank you, Mr. Kruger, for your kind words," said the second little match girl, and her eyes were moist also.

"Now, young lady," continued the Match King, "you must tell me where you are dining this New Year's Eve."

"Why, nowhere," she answered softly, "for I had intended to stay out in the snowstorm until every last match was sold."

"Nonsense!" thundered the old man. "They shall be sold another time. As it happens, I am alone on this festive occasion, passing through Copenhagen on my way to an important business meeting in New York. You shall feast with me tonight on roast goose stuffed with apples and prunes!"

The eyes of the second little match girl shone in anticipation of the toothsome dish. His bearlike arm still around her thin shoulders, the Match King turned toward the brightly lit portals of the hotel. But then something caught his eye, and he stopped.

"Mercy me!" he exclaimed, peering through the blizzard. "Isn't that another little match girl out in the snow?"

"Why, yes!" said the second little match girl. "But she doesn't sell Kruger matches. She works for the competition."

"No matter," he cried merrily. "Tonight we put aside our differences. Tonight all little match girls shall dine off roast goose with the Match King!"

And gesturing to the doorman to fetch the other bare-foot girl, he strode into the hotel. The second little match girl's face showed some displeasure at this turn of events. And the doorman was hard put to persuade the first little match girl to join the festivities, for she was loath to intrude on her fellow salesperson's triumph. But she allowed herself to be led inside, and soon the oddly assorted trio were mounting the majestic marble stairway to the Match King's sumptuous apartments.

Imagine the two little match girls' astonishment at the scene that greeted them! In the center of the dining room of the great man's chambers hung a vast chandelier whose brilliant light was reflected by a thousand exquisite pieces of cut glass. And beneath the chandelier was laid out a feast, upon the likes of which neither girl had ever laid her eyes. Fruits and nuts and special holiday breads were piled high in silver baskets. Hams and other meats glistened as they dripped their juices into silver chargers. Bottles of champagne thrust their colorful heads out of silver buckets. And in the place of honor, right in the midst of that groaning board, nestled on a vast silver plate, was the biggest roast goose they had ever seen, stuffed to bursting with apples and prunes and chestnuts and sausages and spices!

The Match King shrugged out of his huge fur coat, and it was spirited away by a manservant. He sat down happily at the head of the table. The two little match girls awaited his command, their eyes cast shyly down.

"Well, my dears," he said, "before we begin our feast, we must replace these rags with something a little more appropriate. For you, I think," he continued, turning to the second little match girl, "a perky little dirndl. Do you know your bust size?"

"No, Mr. Kruger," she replied demurely. "I have

never had occasion to buy a fitted garment. Besides, I have only recently begun to have a bust as I am but sixteen years of age."

"No matter," said the kindly old man. "We can estimate it manually. Come hither."

"Willingly, sir," said the second little match girl, "but might I trouble you first for a glass of champagne?"

"Mercy me!" chuckled he. "Of course! What an oaf I am!"

With a deft movement he drew the cork from a bottle of champagne and filled three flutes to the brim. He offered one to the second little match girl, who took it eagerly, but when he turned to the first little match girl, she recoiled.

"Thank you, sir, no," she whispered. "For liquor was my father's downfall, and I have vowed that never a drop shall pass my lips."

The second little match girl muttered something under her breath. Then, drawing near to her mentor, she toasted him and drank thirstily.

"Now, dear Mr. Kruger," she said, her eyes wide with interest, "perhaps you'd be so kind as to estimate my bust size."

With trembling hands, the regal old gentleman untied the drawstring at her neck and drew down her ragged bodice to reveal an exquisite white bosom. Despite her somewhat emaciated shoulders, her breasts were full and beautifully curved, each delicate nipple the color of a wild rose. This combination of a thin waifish frame and generous young breasts, so filled, as it seemed, with hope, engaged the old man immensely. Delighted, he cupped the evidence of her womanhood with his hands.

"I'd say you're a medium large," he said. "Now, my

dear," he continued to the first little match girl, "let's do yours."

But the first little match girl, who had been following these activities with horrified eyes, shrank away.

"Oh, no, sir!" she gasped. "No man shall touch me until we have exchanged the most holy vows of matrimony."

"You saucy little witch!" chuckled the Match King. "Making a game of it, are we? Well, I love a little sport. Now, how shall we get that bodice off your little snack tray, *hmmm?*"

And so saying, he rose from his chair to approach her. But the second little match girl restrained him gently and whispered something in his ear. He nodded his assent, and she, taking the first little match girl by the arm, led her into the next room, a splendidly appointed bedchamber.

"Hearken well, dearest," she whispered, "this is an opportunity sent by Providence. There's more at stake than a hot meal and a warm bed. If we work together, we need never sell another match as long as we live!"

Without a word the first little match girl went to the casement and flung open the window. The blizzard had blown away, and the night sky was clear. In the multitudinous heavens, one star shone more brightly than the rest.

"Behold that star," said the first little match girl. "Just seven short days ago it lighted the way to the birth of our beloved Savior."

"I fear you do not quite grasp the situation," said the second little match girl rather sharply. "With only one of us, it's his word against that of a little match girl. With two of us, there's a witness."

Her eyes full of revulsion, the first little match girl

backed away. But her companion turned her gently round toward the window. From where they stood, all Copenhagen was stretched out beneath them. Its roofs and spires and turrets were completely coated with a silver cloak of snow. The old city looked like a magical kingdom.

"Just think, dear friend," whispered the second little match girl, "a few hours' work and all this can be ours."

"Get thee behind me, Satan!" whispered the first little match girl fiercely. "For what doth it profit a man if he gain the whole world, and lose his immortal soul? Matthew 16.26."

"Have it your own way," said the second little match girl, shrugging, and pushed her out the window.

Returning to the dining room, the second little match girl went demurely to her host and stood before him, her charming breasts thrust out proudly.

"Dear Mr. Kruger, I'm afraid our friend has gone home," she said. "I think it just as well, for she wished you ill. I told you she was the competition."

"Why, thank you, little match girl!" exclaimed the Match King. "Take this bauble as a token of my gratitude." And round her slender neck he placed a gorgeous necklace of emerald and gold.

Without further ado, the second little match girl unbuttoned the old man's trousers. Gently she withdrew the scepter of his eminence. Alas, it drooped and shrank from its proper station.

"Ah, my dear, you are kind and full of hope," he said a little sorrowfully. "But it has been ten years since my soldier stood to attention."

"Let me light your fire, Match King," murmured the second little match girl, turning her lustrous blue eyes upward to her sovereign, as she gently took his torch between her even, pearly teeth. Her ruby-red lips rolled softly back and forth, her pink tongue flickering in and out and over and around, like that of a baby bird begging for food. Suddenly fire flared from the old man's eyes. He stiffened—every bit of him!

"Sweet God," he cried. "This hasn't happened since Biarritz in 1883."

Outside, meanwhile, at the mouth of an alley formed by the hotel and the next building, the first little match girl lay buried in a snowdrift.

She could not move, for both her legs were broken.

Oh, how cold it was lying in the snow! Her hands were almost frozen now. Not a soul had she seen or heard since her plunge from the window. There was no one to help her, even though she had fought so valiantly for her virtue. It was late now, and the New Year's revelers were all inside, waiting for the clock to strike twelve. Perhaps if she lit just one of her precious matches, it might warm her hands. She drew one out and struck it against the alley wall. *Whisht!* How it blazed! It gave out a beautiful light, and as she warmed first one hand then the other, it seemed to her as though the match had become a great nickel-plated iron stove, with brass legs, in a cozy old kitchen. So delightfully did it heat the room that the little maiden tried to reach out her feet toward the stove. But they hurt, oh, how they hurt! And lo, the flame went out and the stove vanished and she was back in the drift.

High above her, on the stroke of twelve, the old Match King, rekindled as never before, lay back also—beneath his delightful new friend. What a New Year this would be! And while it might be best to draw a discreet veil over the rest of their joyous endeavors—for things were done that night that had never been done before in Copenhagen—suffice it to say that whenever the second little match girl put her lips to his beacon, she could blow its spark into a roaring blaze. By day's dawning, he had made up in one night for ten years of chilly winter.

Meanwhile, all through New Year's night, the first little match girl lay in the snowdrift, lighting matches to warm her tiny frozen fingers. One match burned with a greenish flame, and she was transported to a store window she had once seen, where a great Christmas tree stood, wax tapers burning on its branches. The tree grew and grew, until it seemed to touch the sky, and the lights became stars, and one of them fell to earth in a long trail of fire.

"Now someone is dying," said the poor child softly. For her grandmother, who was the only person in her life who had shown her love, and who was now dead, had told her that when a soul passes from its mortal shell, a star falls from heaven.

She struck one more match, and her grandmother's dear dead face appeared to her in its light. And lest her grandmother should disappear, she struck the whole bundle of her remaining matches against the wall, and a great light shone out as bright as noonday. Her grandmother stood there alive and lovely.

"Oh, Grandmother, never leave me now!" cried the first little match girl. "Take me to Heaven with you, where I may be happy for all eternity!"

"I cannot, my sweet," said her grandmother. "I'm only a hallucination. All that's left of me is a bag of bones in a rotting pine box held together by a terrible smell. There is no Heaven. To be quite honest, you'd've been better off whipping some skull on the old-timer."

With that her grandmother disappeared, and for the little match girl there was no more cold or hunger or care or woe.

They found her the next morning at the dawn of day, frozen stiff, the bundle of burned matches in her hand.

"Poor little thing," they said. "She tried to warm herself."

No one knew just how bad it had been for the first little match girl. No one, that is, except the second little match girl, who passed by the alley on her way to Copenhagen's most luxurious department store, where she was to buy her very own full-length sable fur coat.

For the Atlantic crossing is cold in winter and it's colder still in New York City.

VII

BLASPHEMY

Blasphemy, the greatest of all vices, the grand opera of Bad Virtue, has fallen into serious disrepair. Blasphemy is a vice of the believer, and if you believe in nothing, you cannot blaspheme.

Blasphemy has been downgraded in a secular age to disrespect. But it was once a dangerous business. Blasphemy is a lot more than dissing the Deity. It is daring the Deity. It's stretching the limits of the Deity's patience. It's like connecting a wire-guidance system from the top of your head to the nearest thunderbolt.

In the days when most people of a given nationality subscribed to pretty much the same set of superstitions, the authorities were well within their mandate if they executed blasphemers. These nuts could bring down major wrath on an innocent public. That was the reasoning behind the Ayatollah's *fatwa* against Salman Rushdie. Conventional PEN-type wisdom casts the death sentence as an offense against some unspecified global version of the First Amendment; the fact is, however, that Rushdie was perfectly aware that *The Satanic Verses* was blasphemous, and the Ayatollah was equally aware that if the blasphemer was allowed to continue living, there was no knowing what else he might write to get up Allah's nose, which is to be praised a thousand thousand times, unto all ages.

143

Kill the bastard, was the thinking, before he kills us.

In our endlessly tolerant society, all the fun's gone out of traditional blasphemy. Written or spoken blasphemy is now interpreted as evidence of some entirely secular disorder. Here's a typical piece of traditional blasphemy:

> Then Jesus took the beloved disciple into the Upper
> Room and caused him to kneel before him, saying:
> Take, eat, for this is My Body.
> Whereat the beloved disciple did as he was bid;
> And afterward they smoked a cigarette.

Latent homosexuality for sure—or long-repressed childhood rage. Certainly not a game of chicken with the Son of God. But that's what it is. And since it was written by a practicing Catholic, the chances are that merely by reading these words, the reader is in serious jeopardy. (Too late now.) *No liability is assumed by either author or publisher should a lump of frozen toilet waste from a passing jet now crash through the roof of the reader and brain him or her; merely by opening this book, the reader has agreed to indemnify author and publisher from all such claims.*

From any point of view except God's, in other words, the blasphemy above is completely harmless. Here's a more effective and modern piece of blasphemy:

> "O Lord!" gasped Minnie as Donald dragged her slim hips forcefully against his straining manroot. "O my true sweet Duck," she breathed as his questing fingers found her soft pliant center. She let herself slip deep into the feathery whiteness of his desire as his hard throbbing length prised open the narrow gates of her hot velvet warmth. Forgotten now her mousy hair, the ears she thought too big, the button nose she hated so; all was

swept away in the wild storm of Donald's engorged maleness; finally he was hers and she was his!

"Dear heart," she whispered as his throbbing shaft propelled her ever closer to the dark moon of ecstasy, "Pluto himself could not take me to such heights!"

"Good God Almighty!" came a reed-thin voice. It was Mickey. The poor creature had torn his clothes from his tiny frame as he entered the bedchamber, so great was his desire for his beloved Minnie. Now he stood naked in the doorway, aghast at the spectacle of his wife spread-eagled beneath his best friend, the pathetic evidence of his need jutting from his puny loins.

The Church of the Holy Rodent is considerably more sacred to most Americans than the Holy Church of Rome. However, none amongst the faithful should be offended, for the above quote is not what it seems. The next paragraph of the romance novel from which it's drawn (*Rip My Bodice Slowly* by Pilar O'Steele, copyright 1993 Lovewet Books) goes as follows:

"Minerva!" screamed the Dowager Duchess, pushing aside her crippled son as she rushed into the bedchamber. "You shameless, wanton hussy!" She tugged helplessly at the brawny gamekeeper who, oblivious in his thrusting passion, still pinned her wayward daughter-in-law to the bed. But it was useless. "Ah, Michael, Michael," she sobbed to her son. "Did I not warn you that marriage to a serving wench would bring disaster to our proud escutcheon?"

Just then, Donald's wife Daisy, the scullery maid, joined the throng, wielding a large skillet. She approached the bed where her husband sat, dazed with unsatisfied desire, and crowned him with it, killing him instantly. Thus concluded the first of the many adulteries of Minerva, Duchess of Ramsbotham.

Latin scholars will realize that "Pluto" is a blasphemy consistent with the lascivious character of Minerva. It refers, of course, to the King of the Underworld. The word "Duck" in the very first paragraph is a typo; it should read "Duke."

The Morning Prayer of Jerry Fallback

Almighty God, under whom we be, shower your bless-ings upon your faithful gathered here and, in your mercy, crush the testicles of our enemies. And when their testi-cles have been reduced to bloody pulp, O Lord, shove the flaming sword of your righteousness up their unholy butts! And churn it round in there, Lord!

For they have sinned in your sight, Lord, but we who beseech you have been cleansed in the blood of the Re-publican Lamb!

And when thou hast reamed them but good, Sweet Savior, in thy infinite love kill the baby killers slowly with bone cancer. Yea, and smash the heads of the bleeding hearts in multiple fiery car wrecks, and chew up the flesh of the drug-crazed Nubians with their own hollow-nose bullets, and shrivel the foul sodomites with the avenging virus of thy retribution!

We give you thanks, Almighty God. You all have a nice day now.

Lives of the Saints—No. 445: Saint Urethra and Saint Colostomy, Martyrs

The *Vitae Sanctorum* has inspired Christians—especially the young—throughout the centuries to ever greater feats of faith.

During the reign of the Emperor Diocletian there dwelt in the province of Phrygidia in Asia Minor a rich merchant named Cephalon. Cephalon had two children, Urethra and Colostomy, a girl and a boy respectively, born within min-utes of each other. In all things the twins emulated one another, so that when Colostomy came under the tutelage of Diode, Bishop of Masochia and converted to Christian-

147

ity, Urethra instantly followed suit. This greatly incensed their father, who still worshipped the pagan goddess Diana. Even in that age of great piety their fellow Christians marveled at the devotion of the young twins to Our Blessed Savior: at their incorruptible virginity and vigilance against the wiles of Satan; at their daily mortification of each other with nail-studded leather whips, soaked in lye.

In the year 303 A.D. Diocletian declared that Christianity was to be eradicated throughout the Roman Empire. The Roman governor of Phrygidia, Appius Phella, sought to implement the imperial decree zealously in his province whereupon Cephalon, to curry favor with the Romans, denounced his own dear children, who were not yet fifteen years of age, to the governor.

The two young Christians were dragged from their devotions to the Roman fort where centurions thrust great funnels into their tender fundaments and poured molten lead therein; at the same time beating their sweet unsullied bodies with bars of iron, pouring acid into their wounds and calling upon them to renounce their faith. Needless to say, this they steadfastly refused to do. Appius Phella, being called to supervise their torment, now ordered that a team of horses rip Urethra's arms and legs from their sockets and that her intimate organs be sliced off, fried in oil and eaten by the soldiers before her eyes; at each turn telling her brother that she would be spared further pain if he would turn his back on his Savior. But his sister forbade him, laughing merrily and crying out that she was glad to be rid of her intimate organs since they but bound her to the ordure of sin. When Appius Phella ordered the same fate for Colostomy he too laughed merrily, as his intimate organs were likewise fried and eaten. For did not each emulate the other in everything? All that remained of the young saints by now were battered, burned, limbless, bleeding, acid-scarred trunks and heads, yet Appius Phella caused their eyes to be gouged out with splintered spear-handles and their bodies ground between great millstones; then he cast them into the ocean so that giant jellyfish would sting them incessantly until they died. The next morning, however, through the grace of God, the waves cast the sightless heads of Urethra and Colostomy, still alive and burning bright with the light of faith, back upon the shore where they recited the Credo joyously in unison until the enraged governor, summoned to witness this miracle, smashed them into pulp with a rock. Thus Christ showed his great love for his young friends in allowing them to earn the ineffable reward of dwelling with Him for all eternity.

A Paternoster for Travelers on USAir

Our Father, who art in the unlikely event of a water landing,
Hallowed be thy name is Sue and in the rear cabin, Carmen.
Thy kingdom comfortably around your waist,
Thy will be taking time to familiarize yourself with the exits on earth as it is two forward exits in heaven.
Give us this day our seat belts lightly at all times,
And forgive us our loss of cabin pressure as we forgive those who must fit under the seats in front of you,
And lead us not into turbulence, but enjoy your flight. Amen.

The Confession of St. Augustine, Florida

Whether the following thrill-packed story can be classified as blasphemy depends somewhat on how much the reader likes the movies of Oliver Stone.

Father Mulcahy checked around the pews once more before he drew the curtain of the confessional. The gentle old Spanish-style church seemed as peaceful as could be

in the late afternoon light, but these days it was decep-
tive. Mary the Immaculate was on the very edge of the
worst part of St. Augustine; he was always rousting
drunks and addicts from the back rows or the steps of
the side altars, where they'd crashed. Mrs. Gomez had
been mugged just last week as she did the Stations of the
Cross, for Godsake. What had happened to that old idea
of sanctuary?

He could leave the curtain open, sure, to keep an eye
on the place. But there was something wrong with that.
The good father was old-fashioned. He believed, unlike
most of his contemporaries, that the sacraments were a
private affair between a man and his God. Especially
confession. People had a right to that drawn curtain.

Only one guy out there. Older man, Hispanic-looking
but probably harmless. Head bent way down in studious
devotion, hands together fervently, unclasped, fingers
pointing north. That usually meant someone who got to
church about once every ten years. Piety remembered
from parochial school. Might be a juicy one. He drew
the curtain.

There it was—the rustle and grunt as a heavy man
knelt opposite him, on the other side of the grille.

"Bless me, father, for I have sinned . . ."

Yup. With that formula this one hadn't been in
church in years. Definitely Hispanic. Could be Cuban.

"It has been many years since last I go to confession.
Maybe . . . thirty, thirty-five . . ."

When he was young, Father Mulcahy might've got a
little twinge of pastoral excitement at this announcement—a black sheep returning to the fold. Experience
had taught him, though, that score-settling confessions
were usually brought about by bad news from the doctor.
He waited for the customary list of adulteries, bad
drunks, petty thefts, fights. But there was only silence.
The man sighed deeply.

"Well?" said the priest. Still nothing.

"What sins do you want to confess . . . er . . . my son?" The older ones liked that. But it didn't help either. The guy was like an oil painting.

"You want to confess sins of the flesh, maybe? Impurities? Women other than your wife?"

"Yes." The man sighed again.

"Anything else?" Silence out there. "You get drunk at all, high, beat your wife?"

"No. No drink. No drugs. No wife."

Impurities, no wife. Father Mulcahy coughed with distaste.

"You—er—swing the other way, perhaps?"

"No."

"How about stealing. Ever steal anything?"

"No."

"So that's it—impurities?" More silence. Irritation swept over the priest. It was late. He wanted to catch the end of the Marlins game.

"You're gonna have to give me a little help here, fella."

Sweet Jesus. The guy was sobbing. Quietly, but he could see the big shoulders heaving through the grille.

"My son, God is good. He wants to forgive you. Whatever you want to say, you can say it here. You are speaking only to God."

"I—" The guy choked.

"Take your time."

"I . . . killed a man."

Well, well. He'd always known it would happen one day. Amazingly, considering the mayhem around him, Father Mulcahy had never heard these words in his confessional. Outside, yes, all the time. But there was always an excuse. He raped my sister; she slept with another guy; it was self-defense. Killing wasn't a sin anymore. It was a no-fault affair, a traffic accident.

"When was this?"

"Many, many years ago."

"Do the police know?"

"No."

"God will forgive you, my son. Even this terrible sin. But for me to give you absolution, you have to go to the authorities and tell them also."

"I—I cannot do that."

"I know it's difficult. But that's the rules. God knows, I'd never tell anyone. But you must."

"It was—the authorities that made me kill the man."

"Well, now. Maybe that's different. Was this in the line of duty, in the military, something like that?"

"No. It was a terrible crime."

The guy was weeping again, great wrenching sobs. Father Mulcahy was getting alarmed. He was a big fella, overweight for sure, sixty if he was a day. Prime heart-attack material.

"So many years . . . hiding . . . running. If I go to authorities, they kill me."

"Okay. Okay, my son. Calm down. Try and tell me what happened and we'll see what we can do."

The guy took a deep breath, but he was still choking as he spoke.

"It was many years ago . . ."

"Yes. Go on. You already told me that."

"I stand on a bridge over a highway with a rifle near a tree. I fire two bullets . . ."

"Yes, yes. At who?"

". . . into the head of the president of the United States."

Father Mulcahy felt like he was on an elevator in free fall. His brain was spinning inside his skull.

"I—I don't believe you."

"Is true . . ." The guy began to weep again. "I . . . am the one . . . they look for all these years . . ."

The tattered White House portrait that used to be behind the cash register in Linehan's Bar and Grill flashed before the old priest's eyes. The thick Irish hair, those fierce Irish eyes. Our young president struck down in the prime of his life . . . God knows he hadn't seen eye to eye with him on anything, except the Bay of Pigs, but he was an Irishman for Chrissake. Blood is blood. And this fucking beaner . . .

He looked with contempt through the grille at the heaving shoulders. Weeping like a goddamn woman. What about little John-John? What about poor little Caroline? What about that beautiful young widow? What've you got to cry about, you fucking spick?

"Father, forgive me, bless me. Give me the *absolvo, por favor* . . ."

"Sure, I'll give absolution, you fucking murderer. You go to hell, my friend."

Father Mulcahy drew the .38 Police Special his brother Kevin gave him on his deathbed and fired two bullets into the head of the killer of the first and only Catholic president of the United States of America.

God and Steven Hawking

I'm terribly sorry, said God to Steve Hawking
—How can I put this with something like tact?—
It was I who created the time-space continuum
And you too, young Steve, as a matter of fact . . .

—————

The Book of Creation

BEING THE TRUE BOOK OF GENESIS ACCURATELY
TRANSLATED FROM THE ORIGINAL DIVINE TEXTS,
BY P. ROBERTSON (© 1994, THE SEND-$6.95 CLUB)

Over millennia the Bible has been transformed by
interpolations—well-meaning or otherwise—inserted into it by
special interests. Liberals, bleeding hearts, sob sisters, Papists,
and other so-called religious groups have all had their way with
the Good Book. Happily, a new breed of scholars is now using
modern technology to strip away this radical crud and bring to
the faithful exactly what the intentions of the Almighty were when
He created the world six thousand years ago.

Chapter The First

IN the beginning God created Dates.

2   And the date was Monday, July 4, 4004 B.C.

3   And God said, Let there be light; and there was light.
And when there was Light, God saw the Date, that it
was Monday, and he got down to work; for verily, he
had a Big Job to do.

4   And God made pottery shards and Silurian mollusks
and pre-Cambrian limestone strata; and flints and
Jurassic Mastodon tusks and Pithecanthropus
erectus skulls and Cretaceous placentals made he;
and those cave paintings at Lascaux. And that was
that, for the first Work Day.

5   And God saw that he had made many wondrous
things, but that he had not wherein to put it all. And
God said, Let the heavens be divided from the earth;
and let us bury all of these Things which we have
made in the earth; but not too deep.

6 And God buried all the Things which he had made, and that was that.

7 And the morning and the evening and the overtime were Tuesday.

8 And God said, Let there be water; and let the dry land appear; and that was that.

9 And God called the dry land Real Estate; and the water called he the Sea. And in the land and beneath it put he crude oil, grades one through six; and natural gas put he thereunder, and prehistoric carboniferous forests yielding anthracite and other ligneous matter; and all these called he Resources; and he made them Abundant.

10 And likewise, all that was in the Sea, even unto two hundred miles from the dry land, called he Resources; all that was therein, like manganese nodules, for instance.

11 And the morning unto the evening had been an long day; which he called Wednesday.

12 And God said, Let the earth bring forth abundantly every moving creature I can think of, with or without backbones, with or without wings or feet, or fins or claws, vestigial limbs and all, right now; and let each one be of a separate species. For lo, I can make whatsoever I like, whensoever I like.

13 And the earth brought forth abundantly all creatures, great and small, with and without backbones, with and without wings and feet and fins and claws, vestigial limbs and all, from bugs to brontosauruses.

14 But God blessed them all, saying, Be fruitful and multiply and Evolve Not.

15 And God looked upon the species he had made, and saw that the earth was exceeding crowded, and he said unto them, Let each species compete for what

it needeth; for Healthy Competition is My Law. And the species competeth amongst themselves, the cattle and the creeping things, the dogs and the dinosaurs; and some madeth it and some didn't, and the dogs ate the dinosaurs, and God was pleased.

16   And God took the bones from the dinosaurs, and caused them to appear mighty old; and cast he them about the land and the sea. And he took every tiny creature that had not madeth it, and caused them to become fossils; and cast he them about likewise.

17   And just to put matters beyond the valley of the shadow of a doubt, God created carbon dating. And this is the origin of species.

18   And in the Evening of the day which was Thursday, God saw that he had put in another good day's work.

19   And God said, Let us make man in our image, after our likeness, which is tall and well-formed and pale of hue: and let us also make monkeys, which resembleth us not but are short and ill-formed and hairy. And God added, Let man have dominion over the monkeys and the fowl of the air and every species, endangered or otherwise.

20   So God created Man in His own image; tall and well-formed and pale of hue created He him, and nothing at all like the monkeys.

21   And God said, Behold, I have given you every herb-bearing seed, which is upon the face of the earth. But ye shalt not smoketh it, lest it giveth YOU ideas.

22   And to every beast of the earth and every fowl of the air, I have given also every green herb, and to them it shall be for meat. But they shall be for you. And the Lord God your Host suggesteth that the flesh of cattle goeth well with that of the fin and the claw, thus shall Surf be wedded unto Turf.

23 And God saw everything he had made, and he saw that it was very good; and God said, It just goes to show Me what the private sector can accomplish. With a lot of fool regulations this could have taken billions of years.

24 And on the evening of the fifth day, which had been the roughest day yet, God said, Thank me it's Friday. And God made the weekend.

Chapter The Second

THUS the heavens and the earth were finished, and all in five days, and all less than six thousand of years ago; and if thou believest it not, in a sling shalt thou find thy hindermost quarters.

2 Likewise God took the dust of the ground, and the slime of the Sea and the scum of the earth and formed Man therefrom, and breathed the breath of life right in his face. And he became Free to Choose.

3 And God made an Marketplace eastward of Eden, in which the man was free to play. And this was the Free Play of the Marketplace.

4 And out of the ground made the LORD God to grow four trees: the Tree of Life, and the Liberty Tree, and the Pursuit of Happiness Tree, and the Tree of the Knowledge of Sex.

5 And the LORD God commanded the man, saying, This is my Law which is called the Law of Supply and Demand. Investeth thou in the trees of Life, Liberty, and the Pursuit of Happiness and thou shalt make for thyself an fortune. For what fruit thou eatest not, that thou mayest sell, and with the seeds thereof expand thy operations.

6 But of the fruit of the Tree of the Knowledge of Sex,

thou mayest not eat, nor mayest thou invest therein, nor profit thereby, nor expand its operations; for that is a mighty waste of seed.

7   And the man was exceeding glad. But he asked the LORD God: Who then shall labor in this Marketplace? For am I not management, being tall and well-formed and pale of hue?

8   And the LORD God said unto himself, Verily, this kid hath the potential which is Executive.

9   And out of the ground the LORD God formed every beast of the field and every fowl of the air and brought them unto Adam to labor for him. And they labored for peanuts.

10   Then Adam was again exceeding glad. But he spake once more unto the LORD God, saying, Lo, I am free to play in the Marketplace of the LORD, and have cheap labor in plenty; but to whom shall I sell my surplus fruit and realize a fortune thereby?

11   And the LORD God said unto himself, Verily, this is an Live One.

12   And he caused a deep sleep to fall upon Adam and he took from him one of his ribs, which was an spare rib.

13   And the spare rib which the LORD God had taken from the man, made he woman. And he brought her unto the man, saying:

14   This is Woman and she shall purchase your fruit, to eat it; and ye shall realize a fortune thereby. For Man produceth and Woman consumeth, wherefore she shall be called the Consumer.

15   And they were both decently clad, the Man and the Woman, from the neck even unto the ankles, so they were not ashamed.

VIII

COLD HARD-HEARTEDNESS

The following story appeared June 7, 1994, in the *New York Post:*

HOW TO GET DISS-CEASED

Call it the Diss of Death.

An accidental shove, a misread look, a grumbled remark. To most city dwellers these are petty aggravations—like getting stuck in a traffic jam. But to a growing number of street toughs they've become reasons to kill. They call it being "dissed"—short for disrespected.

- George Todd, a 65-year-old retired Marine, fatally shot in the head outside a Bedford Stuyvesant store where he'd been shopping for his dinner. Todd had accidentally bumped into someone in the store.

- Rashad King, 16, shot and killed while returning to Brooklyn on the F train. The motive: one of his friends had looked at a teen gang member "the wrong way."

- At least four people stabbed this past winter as they walked along Manhattan streets. Motive: they all bumped accidentally into Darryl Wright, who told police "I'm tired of being disrespected."

The story continues with more examples of dissing and tips on how to go about getting killed for bumping into someone or catching their eye.

> "Step on someone's sneakers and you'll get killed. That's the way it is in the 'hood." Dawan Dimmock, teenager.
>
> "She took my comb and never gave it back."
> "Maybe you should cut the bitch." Conversation overheard at Broadway and 96th Street.
>
> "The last person who 'dissed' me is now deceased." "Derrick," a Bronx teenager.

The phenomenon of "dissing" isn't, of course, restricted to the inner city. It's just as likely to happen in a suburban school, in the mall, or for that matter on the highway. People have paid the ultimate penalty on many occasions for a less than enthusiastic glance (or an overly enthusiastic one) as well as for the inadvertent bump on the street, the ill-advised cutting-in on the off-ramp, and so on—all minuscule infractions of the new, harsh, albeit somewhat shadowy code of "respect."

Clearly this changes traditional notions of social intercourse. No more cheery greetings to strangers on a sunny morning. No more offers to help old ladies across the street, no more polite smiles as you make way for the infirm or less fortunate, no more asking for directions or giving them, no more interest in people at work or even in parents playing with their kids. Avert your eyes, turn the cold shoulder, harden your heart, listen to no one, respond to nothing, hurry on. Helpfulness is death. Where possible, carry more firepower than you're likely to encounter. The Glock is easy to conceal—Uzis also, though they tend to overheat. The Desert Special has a lot of stopping power. Steer clear of TEC-9s—they jam. In the nineties these are the basic rules of good manners.

Despite this reality, there's been a great deal of pipe-sucking pontification by neo-Victorians about how salutory it would be for the nation if we would start treating one another again with good old-fashioned courtesy. Allan Bloom led the charge with *The Closing of the American Mind,* and the good-manners movement has a rightish tinge (Emmett Tyrell, Jr., most of *Commentary,* most of *The National Review,* Hilton Kramer), but it's increasingly across the political board: Paul Fussell, Tom Wolfe, James Lincoln Collier.

Some might feel that deploring bad manners borders on un-Americanism since a demotic lack of couth has always been one of the things that made Americans attractive vis-à-vis the rest of the world. More to the point, bad manners take on a different tone when they're being expressed with a .357 Magnum 180-grain Winchester Black Talon.

Nonetheless, the graybeards persist. Here's an example of the kind of traditional "character-building values" neo-Victorians feel would have prevented Darryl Wright from stabbing four people, Rashad King's murderers from shooting him in the back, and Derrick from killing the last person who dissed him. It's from Chapter One (Self-Discipline) of *The Book of Virtues* by William Bennett:

BOY WANTED
by FRANK CRANE (circa 1900)

Wanted—. . . A boy whose fingernails are not in mourning, whose ears are clean, whose shoes are polished, whose clothes are brushed, whose hair is combed, and whose teeth are well cared for; . . .

A boy who whistles in the street, but does not whistle where he ought to keep still;

A boy who looks cheerful, has a ready smile for everybody, and never sulks; . . .

A boy who does not smoke cigarettes and has no desire to learn how; . . .

A boy that never bullies other boys nor allows other boys to bully him; . . .

A boy who looks you right in the eye and tells the truth every time; . . .

A boy who would rather lose his job or be expelled from school than to tell a lie or be a cad;

A boy whom other boys like;

A boy who is not goody-goody, a prig, or a little pharisee, but just healthy, happy, and full of life. . . .

And so on. God help this kid if he ever shows his face in Bed-Stuy.

The Lives of the Saints—
The Singing Nun

This edifying story demonstrates beautifully how well a strict religious upbringing, free of what worldly people call "street smarts," prepares you for the vicissitudes of real life.

Sister Sourire, the Singing Nun, had a runaway hit on Philips Records with "Dominique" in 1963. The song's success was a surprise to her convent in Belgium. In the U.S. the paean to Saint Dominic was simultaneously number one on *Billboard*'s single and album charts. Sister Sourire—her religious name was actually Sister Luc-Gabrielle—subsequently did a seven-month-long nation-wide tour. It was her first taste of what the world had to offer—as opposed to the joys of poverty, discipline, and obedience she was used to in the cloister.

Reports of heavy drinking and marijuana use began to circulate toward the end of the tour, which began with an appearance at Loyola, migrated to the West Coast, and then finished with a huge concert at Notre Dame. Several dates were canceled during the tour for unexplained reasons; this was due to Sister Luc-Gabrielle's being, as one member of her backup group put it, "permanently zonked." The final Notre Dame concert was canceled after a private performance for the Notre Dame faculty, prominent alumni, and other Catholic notables, including the then attorney general, Robert Kennedy. During the show Sister Luc-Gabrielle began to insult the audience, at one point mumbling the Rite of Exorcism in Latin at the president's brother. She then launched into an ultra-up-tempo version of her hit, screaming the chorus, "Dominique, nique, nique, etc.," over and over, progressively louder and more off-key. Finally she threw up into her guitar and left the stage.

Her superiors attributed these lapses to a lack of familiarity with *"tentations mondiales"* (worldly temptations), but her return to the cloister was a stormy one. Some of the episodes of disobedience were trivial. Some were not. For example, it was the custom at her convent for the nuns to be allowed a glass of wine for dinner on their saint's day (the feast day of the saint whose name each had assumed upon taking her final vows). Sister Luc-Gabrielle reportedly began to agitate for: A. a nun being allowed to have as many glasses of wine as she wanted on her saint's day, and B. *all* the sisters being allowed to have as many glasses of wine as they wanted on *anyone's* saint's day. When this campaign failed, she privately sent a circular letter to all the major *négociants* in Bordeaux, Burgundy, Champagne, and the Beaujolais, stating that her order was upgrading its sacramental wine and requesting samples. The *négociants* responded enthusiastically, and she amassed a fair cellar—including many first growth and Grand Cru wines of the excellent '59 vintage—before she was found out.

She quarreled violently with the Mother Superior General of her order over distribution of royalties from "Dominique," demanding that a portion be set aside for "R&D" on future albums. This was refused point-blank, on the grounds of her vow of poverty. It later emerged that she had set up a bank account in California during her U.S. tour and roughly sixty percent of her BMI payments were being channeled there, instead of to the order's orphanages for Thalidomide babies. Another source of friction was that she neglected her religious duties, spending most of her time trying to compose a satisfactory follow-up to "Dominique." She recorded a song dedicated to Saint Benedict entitled "Benedicte"—very similar to her first—but the order objected to its release on the grounds that the first line of the chorus, "Benedicte, dicte, dicte, dicte," might strike English ears as inappropriate. She also insisted on being addressed as "Sister Sourire," demanding that people smile when they did so. Finally she bombarded GMA, her American agency, with demands that she be allowed to join the group Peter, Paul and Mary, apparently under the impression that the names referred to the first two Apostles and the mother of Christ.

In 1966, right after a movie of her life starring Debbie Reynolds bombed, she traveled from the convent to the Vatican, where she requested a private audience with Pope Paul VI. At the audience she informed His Holiness that the huge success of her song and album had been a major contributory factor in "selling" the reforms of Vatican II to the faithful and proposed that an entire order of singing nuns be established with herself as the Mother Superior General. When this request was denied, she became abusive, calling Pope Paul *"un pédé"* (homosexual). According to Vatican sources who escorted her from the papal chambers, she appeared to be under the influence of some unspecified substance.

The ambitious proposal—along with her outrageous behavior—was, of course, more a cry for help than a real plan. A break with the order was inevitable. Quitting it the same year, she made straightaway for the U.S. and specifically San Francisco: the place to be in the midsixties if you had musical ambitions. She resumed her lay name—Jeanine Deckers—and moved in with another musician, a heroin addict named Rex Reinhardt. Then she embarked on what would become a lifelong search for another hit.

There were two obstacles to that dream. First, she'd already topped the charts, and there's nothing so cold as an old hit. (When she announced with great fanfare to the press in June 1966 that "The Singing Nun was going electric," it garnered not a single line of copy anywhere in the continental United States.) Second, it seemed that no matter how hard she rebelled, however bohemian a life she led, she could not conceptually escape from her religious training. This kept her creatively out of step with an ever more secular audience that, if it was religious at all, looked to the East rather than to Rome. Photos of her taken at the time show a conventional hippie with flowers in her waist-length hair—albeit somewhat older than her fellow peace-and-lovers. The first band she tried to form with her rapidly dwindling funds was called *The Summa of Love.* Few people got its reference to the work of the great Dominican saint Thomas Aquinas; most interpreted it as a crassly exploitative misspelling.

The band bombed disastrously, as did two others she formed: *The Dominican Invasion* (1968) and *The Perpetual Light Orchestra* (1969), whose demise was hastened by its unfortunate acronym—PLO. Another ill-advised project involved a lawsuit she brought against the producers of *The Flying Nun;* she claimed to be working on a rock musical of the same name that she had conceived the year before while on an acid trip. (The suit was thrown out of court.) The political side of the Bay Area's counterculture seems largely to have passed her by, but her super-saccharine background gave her a perverse cachet in San Francisco's burgeoning erotic demimonde. (Not dissimilar to the notoriety achieved by porno-queen Marilyn Chambers, who had once been the 99 and 44/100ths percent pure Ivory Soap Girl.) Part of that world was the Hell's Angels biker gang to which she was briefly drawn and whose nonreligious nature she typically misunderstood. She had a tempestuous fling with the Angels' legendary leader, Sonny Barger. However, the experiences gave her an abiding love of Harley-Davidsons; she became a familiar sight in North Beach, riding her "Hog of God," resplendent in black leather and the nun's wimple she had once again taken to wearing. She was known to biker friends as Mama Superia.

More ominously, she was arrested in early 1971 for soliciting; by now her addiction to heroin cost her five hundred dollars a day. This didn't faze her: she referred to her jones as "a nun's habit." She achieved a curious equilibrium in the excitement of San Francisco's ultra-permissive early seventies erotic underground, and she eventually settled on S&M as her "thing." At this she acquired great prominence. Underground publications carried ads for her services promising "strict discipline" and guaranteeing "total obedience"—the old familiar echo of her religious training. She displayed her charms in knee-high spiked-heel black leather boots, a heavily studded black-leather corset, and full-face black leather mask topped off with the trademark nun's wimple. She worked under various pseudonyms, e.g., "Dominique the Dominatrix" and "The Bride of Christ Almighty," but most notably as "Sister Mary Quite Contrary."

She came to look back on this period as the happiest time of her life. But its end came abruptly. In March 1976 one of her regular clients suffered a massive heart attack *in medias res*. The man, a prominent California Republican, member of the Bohemian Club, and intimate of Governor Reagan, was of Scottish extraction and enjoyed being crucified in the manner of Saint Andrew—upside-down on an X-shaped cross. Equipped with a small silver-handled cat-o'-nine-tails, the dominatrix was busy disciplining the "saint" for his imperfections at golf when he went into cardiac arrest; he was amply proportioned, and she couldn't get him down from the cross in time to administer CPR. Luckily for her, the man's position ensured that the case never got to trial, but from then on the SFPD harassed Sister Mary Quite Contrary as mercilessly as she had once flogged her clients.

The beginning of the eighties found her reembarking on a musical career. Although she might have become a beneficiary of nostalgia for the early sixties, which was chic at the time, she instead opted for R&B, on the odd theory that since R&B had religious roots, she was uniquely qualified to interpret it. She scraped together the money for a demo album—a dozen covers of standards by Otis Redding, B.B. King, Muddy Waters, and others, in her unvarying, squeaky "Dominique" monotone. Record producers who heard it said every song was pitched an octave higher than they'd ever heard it before. She insisted on titling the demo "Our Lady Sings the Blues." There were no takers.

She tried a few more harebrained schemes—for example, she campaigned vigorously to become the "voice" of Domino's Pizza—but, as so often before, no one but she saw the appropriateness of the connection. In 1982 she moved back to Belgium, where she shared a house with a friend. According to neighbors, the two women did little but eat, watch television, and drink *kriek*, a cherry-flavored beer. In April 1985 police found the two friends dead, apparently the victims of a massive binge. At the time of her death, the Ex-singing Ex-nun, as she called herself, weighed more than three hundred kilos.

MORAL

Nuns are for the most part idiots.

A Tale of Two Cities

In which we learn that you can prove almost anything with some nifty moral footwork.

"Washit ma'."

"Washyo' ecco ma'."

Jason couldn't help watching either. The big guy with Rasta hair—what did they call those things again? Wow, Marley had been dead a looong time—was wrestling lazily on the streetcorner with a little boy. Perhaps four years old. His? Who knows? Does it really matter? Cute, cute kid. He smiled.

"Fugu laffnat, mofuk?" said the Rasta to Jason.

"Hey," said Jason, smiling, shaking his head. "I've got two little boys too, somewhere in this city. I see a dad having good times with his kid, why that's just the only thing in this whole world I really care about."

"Fugoffaggit," said the Rasta's little boy.

It hit Jason like a cut-down baseball bat in the face. He checked himself, took a deep centering breath. Don't make a big thing of it. Talk to them like adults. Kids need that.

"Hey, don't call people faggots, okay?"

The Rasta had the little boy's head in a headlock. He twisted it hugely, pretending to screw it off. The little boy giggled. Neither responded. Jason felt a twinge of triumph, and immediately regretted it. He wasn't trying to score points after all. He was trying to—

"Gifukoudahood," the Rasta said into the little boy's nappy head.

Jason wasn't sure he'd heard it right.

"Get out of the neighborhood? This is my neighborhood too. That's kinda my point, I guess."

The Rasta said nothing. He went on growling at the little boy's skull. Jason fought the swelling anger.

"I don't believe this city. You reach out a hand to another man. And he knocks it down."

"Chufukoff?" The Rasta locked eyes with Jason, chomping on the kid's hair.

"You know how this started? I had the temerity, the fucking temerity, to smile at another human being. Jesus."

"Dissn me, mofuk?"

"Dissin', you say? No, man. I ain't 'dissin' ' you. Quite the contrary."

He laughed his hollow laugh—the one he'd used when Susan walked out. He shook his head. He turned away.

"Hey! Usay ugo' kiz?"

Jason stopped. What a city! Up, down, up, down! Had he been a shit? Yes, probably. Did it matter? He'd find out. He turned back again.

"Yeah, man, I do." He chuckled dad-to-dad.

"Asscool."

Tears pricked behind Jason's eyelids.

"Two of the cutest—"

The Rasta pulled an Uzi from his jacket, aimed it at Jason's heart . . .

OPTIONAL MORAL ENDING #1

. . . and shot Jason seven times in the chest. Then he stood over him and emptied the rest of the clip into his head. The little boy whooped. His dad picked him up, put him on his shoulders, and ambled round the corner into the night.

OPTIONAL MORAL ENDING #2
. . . and fired one round. The shot missed. Jason held up his hand, laughing.

"Hey, man," he said. "You'd have a much cooler perspective on all this if you were better read. Take Aristophanes, for instance. He lived two thousand five hundred years ago, but his view of the human comedy is as relevant today as it was then. Check this out."

He pulled a copy of *The Frogs* from his backpack. The Rasta pocketed his piece and opened the book at random. Soon he was chuckling away. Their spat forgotten, Jason and the Rasta—whose name was Marten—went off for a beer, and talked for hours about the civilizing influence of the arts. They became fast friends, and Jason later married Marten's sister Kendra.

A Complete Guide to U.S. Foreign Policy

BY WILLIAM JEFFERSON CLINTON

Talk softly and carry a Big Mac.

The Lion and the Mouse

FROM TALES BY ASSOP

This ancient fable teaches us that while nice guys may not always finish last, they often get finished first.

A mighty lion lay asleep in the sunshine. A little mouse, confused by the sunlight, ran upon his paw and wakened him. The lion was just going to eat the little mouse, when it cried: "Oh, please, great mighty Mr. Lion, let me go, sir, please, please, please don't eat me, and I swear upon my little mouse mother's grave that someday, somehow, somewhere I will help you—colossal and mighty and magnificent and infinitely wiser and bigger than me though you be and that—"

"For Chrissake, shut up!" said the lion and went back to sleep.

Not long after that the lion became caught in a hunter's net. He pulled and tugged this way and that, but the ropes were too strong. He began roaring with anger, and the sound thundered through the forest. The little mouse heard him and ran to where he was.

"Be still, O mighty Mr. Lion sir, and I will set you free, just as I swore I would upon my beloved little mouse mother's grave, God rest her soul, in return for your great and overwhelming kindness in setting me free when you had me in your inestimable power—"

"Quit jabbering and get on with it," shouted the lion.

With his sharp little teeth the mouse gnawed through the ropes and set the lion free.

"There you are, mighty Mr. sir Lion sir, and you

probably thought I was too small to do you a good turn. Yet now you owe your life to a poor little mouse who—"

The lion caught the little mouse in his jaws and crunched him up. Just before he got its head, the little mouse sobbed with its dying breath:

"Why? Why, Mr. noble Lion sir, did you consume me even though, contrary to the usual rules of nature, red in tooth and claw, I helped a fellow animal in distress in return for the kindness you showed me? Wasn't there some intrinsic pact here, some moral burden upon you to—"

"Shaddup!" said the lion, swallowing the head. He burped and lay down. He'd get the hunter when he came to check the net. Chew the bastard's arms and legs off. Leave him to die slowly in the sun. Later on, he'd hump that slinky number he'd seen down by the watering hole. Still, what a day! Jeez.

Guns

Guns don't kill people, postal workers kill people.

The Tale of Flavinius and the Syrian

FROM *I CLAUDIUS, YOU JANUS* BY ROBERT O'GRAVES

This important story from the height of the Roman Empire teaches us that to get ahead we must sometimes put our mouth where our money is.

Flavinius was a familiar figure in and around the Forum during the reign of Nero. Not a liked figure certainly, but one who was tolerated because of his usefulness. Flavinius was a broker, a middleman for almost any transaction under the sun, whether it involved grain or hides or household tools or sacred figures. Whenever a merchant or private citizen had some commodity he was having difficulty selling, he would approach Flavinius to find him a buyer; conversely, someone in need of a particular commodity might seek him out to find an available supply. Usually he would charge a commission to one side or the other, but in some happy circumstances—usually involving arms—where each side came to him separately, he was able to extract commissions from both. A far higher commission obviously could be charged when the transaction involved a degree of shadiness—when, for example, a sale broke some law of the Senate. To protect both himself and the Romans he most often represented, Flavinius ranged far afield, seeking buyers and sellers in other cities and settlements, and even occasionally in the farthest-flung provinces of the Empire.

Flavinius, in short, was a kind of parasite, a necessary evil. Because no one had contact with him unless he had that person at a disadvantage, he was universally resented. Since he was also by nature shifty, slippery, and obsequious, it's fair to say that most who had dealings with him despised him. Still he flourished, for he would do anything to close a sale for his clients.

On one occasion Flavinius was approached by an illustrious member of the Senate. The matter was delicate, for this worthy—an inveterate gambler—had won from the idiot son of one of the proconsuls a fine stable of chariot horses. The horses could not be sold in Rome nor even in the neighboring provinces for they were well known, and if the proconsul found out, he would demand that they be returned to the simpleton. They would have to be sold abroad. But this was most dangerous, for Roman law in those days forbade, under the penalty of death, the sale of such animals—which could be used in battle—to any person who might oppose the imperium. And in those troubled times, all foreigners were potential rebels.

Clearly the Senator could have nothing to do with this transaction, since he himself had voted for the law. Accordingly, he offered a colossal commission—three times the usual amount.

First, Flavinius had to spirit the beasts out of the city. He arranged for the proconsul's stables to catch fire and for the horses to perish in the conflagration. In reality, of course, the real horses were driven out of the city ahead of time and broken nags substituted to die in their stead.

Having secreted the horses in Capri, Flavinius now approached a Syrian merchant, with whom he had previously done business, to transport the teams to North Africa, where they would command astronomical prices. The Syrian, knowing the penalties involved, was reluctant. So Flavinius resolved to bring him to Rome, where he might drink deeply of its pleasures at the broker's expense and thus be wooed into an agreement.

On the appointed day, having shown his guest the splendors of the Roman theater and the Roman games, Flavinius arranged an intimate dinner at his house on the Via Appia, for himself, the Syrian, and a bewitchingly beautiful slave girl, whose services he had procured for the night. The girl, whose mistress insisted she was a virgin—a common claim made for top-quality whores in those days—was a trifle stupid. But she seemed to understand what was expected of her, and throughout the meal the Syrian could not tear his eyes away from her. He readily agreed to the terms of the arrangement, and a delighted Flavinius led them both to a sumptuous bed-chamber, where matters might take their course.

He had retired to his private courtyard for a last cup of wine and pleasant contemplation of the killing he was about to make, when he heard his name being bellowed throughout the house. Hurrying back to the bedchamber, he found the slave girl seated upon the bed with the furious Syrian standing over her, buck naked, his large member extremely erect.

"What are you playing at, Flavinius?" he yelled. "I ask the moron here to blow me, and she hasn't a clue what to do!"

Flavinius, baffled by this turn of events, looked questioningly at the whore, who smiled sweetly back at him.

"Watch!" commanded the Syrian, gesturing to the girl. Obediently she knelt before him, took his huge member in her slender hand, and, placing her lips very gently to its head, blew on it.

"Is this some kind of stupid Roman joke?" bellowed the Syrian. "If it is, you can forget—"

Flavinius held up his hand to placate his guest. He knelt down beside the girl.

"Watch carefully," he said to her sternly. "I'm only going to do this once."

———

The Ballad of Arnold and Maria

Yesterday upon the stair
I met a man with rotting hair.
He seized me by the shoulder tight;
He was a most unwelcome sight.

"Forgive me er, stranger," quoth this dude.
"I've no intention to be er rude;
For one brief hour I er quit my crypt,
For I am by a question gripped.

"The answer to it you may er know;
With vigor yield it up if so:
How did that Austrian conniver,
Arnold, snag Maria Shriver?"

Relief now flooded through my brain,
For to the ghoul I could explain
An answer I myself had sought
One evening at Hyannisport.

"America's First Family
Worries for its longevity;
They need to breed," I said, "in truth—
A Kennedy who's bulletproof."

———

Another Tale of Two Cities

It was a thick, sticky Manhattan summer night. Henry drove the Range Rover nice and easy up Lenox Avenue, windows down, tape player blaring Brahms's Second Piano Concerto at its ear-splitting max. Justin took the chilled '84 Meursault from a bucket between them and poured Henry a glass. Henry sipped it, then scowled with dissatisfaction.

"Too hot for Burgundy," he muttered, pulling the Range Rover over to the corner of 126th Street. A crack dealer stood there, hands in floppy hip-hop jacket: big kid, micro-short hair with a lightning flash carved into it. He sized up the two honkies.

"Hey, dude!" Henry bellowed over the Brahms. "Know where I could buy a bottle of Condrieu round here? Prefer '88, but '89 would do."

The crack dealer strained to hear what Henry was saying. "Turnat fugashitdown," he yelled.

"Condrieu," Henry yelled back. "Viognier. Wine. From the northern Rhone Valley. South of where this comes from." He held up the half-full glass of Meursault and pointed to it helpfully.

A black top-down Samurai with four guys in it, two in the back, two in the front, all with micro-short haircuts and things carved into them, pulled up on the passenger side of the Range Rover. Justin waved gaily at the newcomers. "Hey, dudes, whassup?" he yelled.

The driver leaned out of the Samurai. He was the biggest of the four. He stared murder at Justin, baring his teeth slightly. One of them was gold—the same color as the Range Rover's hubcaps. The muzzle of a TEC-9 slid discreetly out the back window.

"Turnat fugashitdown," he hissed.

"The music? Oops. Sorry." Justin smiled apologetically and snapped the Brahms tape out of the player and slapped another in. Handel pounded through the intersection. Someone inside the car said something to the driver.

OPTIONAL MORAL ENDING #1

"Turnat fugashitdown mofuk," repeated the driver.

Henry slammed the Range Rover into reverse, screeching back several yards. Justin pulled out his Glock and sprayed the Samurai from what was now a vantage point, killing three of its occupants instantly. The driver, shot but not dead, half-fell from the car and tried to crawl clear. Henry drove forward over him, crushing his head. The crack dealer, mesmerized by these developments, now turned to run. Henry pulled up the Street-Sweeper and pumped four shells into the left side of his jacket. He crumpled on the sidewalk, his heart turned to hamburger. The two honkies hi-fived. Justin cut the Handel. The Range Rover, lights doused, purred off up 126th, heading east.

OPTIONAL MORAL ENDING #2

"Thass better," said the driver, grinning. "Can't stand those late Romantics." The TEC-9 disappeared inside the car, and it drove away.

"Care for a drink?" asked Henry, handing the crack dealer a fresh glass of the Meursault. He sipped it cautiously.

"Fine!" he said. "Oh, that is fine. I get a little spice in there, with hints of citrus. Plus it don't make me homicidal like rock do."

"You have a real good palate," said Justin, laughing. "Sure you haven't tasted this before?"

"Nope," said the crack dealer. "But I have found myself a new métier. Thanks, dudes." And by Christmas he was the sommelier at Lutèce.

IX

SEXING AND DRUGGING

We know drugs are illegal. As of course they should be. What possible fun could they be, if they weren't? Who would bother to suck clouds of acrid smoke into their lungs, sniff abrasive acidic crystals into the sensitive linings of their nostrils, or ram a razor-sharp needle into their veins if they hadn't been told not to? The actual physiological effects of, say, marijuana are about as much fun as doing figure eights upside down in a rickety biplane. The real pleasure lies in the knowledge that you and your companion(s) are infinitely smarter than those who are trying to stop you. Clearly they—whether they're parents, Guardian Angels, or former drug czars—are morons, because here you are smoking away and there they are, unable to do a damn thing about it.

Which is why we welcome the current attempts to make sex illegal too. Many cultural strands are coming together here, from all sides of the political mandala. They have in common the belief that sex is bad for you, because it's one or more of the following things: unhealthy, immoral, dangerous, offensive, violent, victimizing, obsolete, unnecessary, uncomfortable, embarrassing, icky, or uncool. Antisex forces make strange bedfellows (if you can forgive such an un-Christian and phallocentric term). There are traditionalists who find the mere image of an engorged penis or glistening vulva so terrifying that they want it removed from the very realm of thinkability. The most obvious voices of this fear are religious—the Rev. Wildmon, the Rev. O'Connor; the less obvious are feminist—Catherine MacKinnon, Andrea Dworkin. Radical feminism is nowhere more neo-Victorian than in its conviction that every penis on the planet is in a permanent state of engorgement, while only oppressed or unenlightened (in other words non-white, working-class) vulvas glisten. Even moderate down-to-earth feminists now seem to accept the axiom that sex is something men cannot do without, but women have no time for; that it's of negligible interest compared to, say, getting into The Citadel. Hence the campaign to banish the very word "sex," with its fearful connotations of engorged or glistening organs, in favor of the word "gender," which denotes only vague and eradicable things like income differential and upper-body strength. The campaign is officially successful (e.g., in federal documents), but its effect on fiction has yet to be examined:

> Willie and Patricia careened madly down the beach, burning with desire. The Florida moon seemed hotter than the midday sun. They tore the flimsy clothing from each other's bodies, groping blindly as they fell to the sand, where, sprinkled by the spume of the pounding surf, they had wild, passionate gender.

Feminist efforts to recriminalize sex do allow one exception: same-sex sex (or rather, same-gender gender). For some reason, when engorged penis meets engorged penis, or one glistening vulva says howdy to another, the occasion is loudly celebrated. Good health and best wishes to all concerned, of course, and long may they enrage both the mealymouthed Mud-dweller of Mississippi and the fulminating Pharisee of St. Patrick's; still, there does seem to be a certain double standard at work. If we're going to get some zing back into sex, we need to get all gender and genders back in the closet—not just the Mom-and-Pop kind.

Which brings us to safe sex. Although fewer people succumb to AIDS each year than die in accidents involving household appliances, the nation writhes in a paroxysm of masochistic prurience, its wrists lashed to the antique bedposts of abstention and onanism. This is excellent. No self-respecting movement to repress sex can get far without a robust incurable disease to give it teeth. A century ago, when those stern values reigned for which we now feel such yearning, society was similarly obsessed by STDs. Nineteenth-century morality sprang as much from fear of venereal disease, especially syphilis, as it did from any urge to sainthood. Like HIV, syphilis could lie dormant in its primary and secondary forms for years; like AIDS, its final—tertiary—stage was a drop-dead killer. Like AIDS, fewer people were actually at risk than were perceived to be. But for the Victorians it was disease not divinity that sat like a buzzard on the shoulder of the chaperone and hovered over the House of Fallen Women.

Armed with such weapons, Victorians did a better job of repressing sex than anyone in history. Since Victorians are being held up as our cultural and moral exemplars in every other area of human conduct, it makes sense that we emulate them sexually. Nothing wrong with that. Victorian sex was deliciously furtive, frilly, sniggering, unhealthy, and wicked. And therefore enormous fun. The tighter you tamp the powder, the bigger the bang.

So in a neo-Victorian era we could expect growing concealment and condemnation—public penalties for a glimpse of stocking. But here's the paradox: Instead of bustles, chaperones, and horsewhipping, we have microskirts, bustiers, underwear as outerwear, Anna Nicole Smith in a tank top, and Tommy Hilfiger's unbuttoned pants. Whassup?

Whassup is probably the most potent force against sex in contemporary society—fashion. Fashion—for centuries an intrinsic part of the courting ritual, an invitation to sex—has now replaced it. Like tattooing, body piercing, and weight training, modern fashion is auto-erotic. (And safe, to boot.) Armani jackets and Hugo Boss slacks are simply not engorged-penis-friendly. Those Diesel jeans make no one's vulva glisten—except perhaps your own.

Plus, of course, when people have sex, it's traditional to remove your clothes. Who in their right minds would want to remove such spectacularly cutting-edge duds? You can have wild passionate gender in Doc Martens if you really must, but it's way cooler to keep dancing.

It isn't the Christian right or the loopy-fem left or even AIDS that's the problem. If we ever want to have great sex again, we're going to have to get out of those clothes.

The Ballad of Ted Bundy

This popular little ditty illustrates that good manners often maketh the man. In fact, they often maketh him a stone killer.

When little Ted
Was called to bed,
He always acted right.
He kissed his Ma
And then his Pa,
And wished them both good night.
He made no noise,
Like naughty boys,
But gently up the stairs
Directly went
When he was sent
And aways said his prayers.

Now bigger, Ted
When called to bed
Still always acted right.
He strangled sluts
And chewed their butts,
But always said "good night."
He made no noise,
Like naughty boys,
Just quietly down the stairs
Directly went
When he was spent
Thus ending the affair.

Yet older, Ted
Became in bed
A trifle less polite.
His sluts he'd slice
And chop and dice,
But still he said "good night."
He made no noise,
Like other boys;
Downstairs he never ran;
No—on tiptoe
He'd quietly go,
The perfect gentleman!

———

The Castaways

This rollicking saga has been told ever since it first appeared in
the eighteenth century. Never in all that time has a woman
understood it.

Betimes there were two Cornish sailor Boys of rough de-
meanour named Matt and Jack. In the spring of 17— the
lads signed on to ply passage in a three-master twixt
Trinidad and The Hague. The ship put in at Martinique
for water ere She crossed the wide Ocean; there, too,
came aboard Madame de Pompadour, mistress of King
Louis of France, and her several maidservants. The fair
Madame, who had been paying a visit to a wealthy land-
owner on that island, was now bound for the court of
Paris and the arms of her Royal Lover. Known throughout Christendom as the most beauteous Creation of a
Wise and Artful Deity, her Ladyship sought to disguise
her charms behind a Veil, which she wore night and day.

Yet were the two young Cornishmen not taken in by this Ruse; they knew her for whom she might be. Daily as they went about their tasks aboard Ship, swabbing the decks or aloft in the rigging, their Thoughts were all upon the fair Lady and how they might Despoil her.

A day out from New Providence a great Storm arose and broke the Ship in a multitude of Pieces. All hands were lost save Matt and Jack, who clung to a shattered Spar and thereby came to the strand of a small isle. Recovering their Spirits next morning, they set out to acquaint themselves with their new Home; the which they found to be utterly deserted save for the lovely person of Madame de Pompadour, insensible and prone, in the wreckage of a small Skiff.

Temptation thus placed in their way, Matt, the coarser of the two, was for spreading the lady's nether portions and Rogering her, insensible or no. Jack, however, being the more seasoned, counseled otherwise. Nurse her back to Health, reasoned Jack, and let gratitude take its Course. Where Force would be met with Contempt and Anger, Kindness might be rewarded with those Services in which the lady most Excelled. They could Roger her now but 'twould be Once and Once only; help her and they might Roger her till Kingdom Come.

Jack's wise counsel prevailed, and the Succor of the two Tars was repaid a thousandfold. For not only was the fair creature filled with gratitude at their Attentiveness; but they were Strapping Lads and she was a Lusty young Maiden who loved Nothing better than to Roger like a rabbit. Ere a day had passed, Matt and Jack were Rogering the King of France's Property without surcease. They Rogered on the silver sand; they Rogered in the greenery. They Rogered in mango trees; they Rogered in sylvan pools. They Rogered her upright, they Rogered her flat;

they Rogered her from the front and the back. Oh, how they Rogered her! And she, being adept at Rogering, used her French wiles to bring Satisfaction to each, Rogering now one, now the other, so that not a Pang of jealousy passed between them. For their part, dining off the lush fruits and fine game in which the isle abounded and drinking their fill of Creation's most beauteous damsel, the two Jolly Rogers believed they had found Eden anew.

Anon, however, after months of such sport, Jack became pensive. While his zest for Rogering slackened not a jot, something there was that was lacking. One day as Matt slept off his Roger-After-Breakfast, and Madame turned her attentions to Jack, he restrained her. Prithee, Madame, saith Jack, I wouldst thee do me a Great Honor. Take the britches and jerkin of Matt here and do you put them on and tie up your hair under his cap. Then walk a ways with me along the strand and do you answer only to the name Derek.

The good Madame, well versed in the ways of the world, and in Particular of the English, readily complied. Having donned the britches and jerkin of the sleeping Tar, she asked only, who might be Derek? The other replied that Derek was his Best Friend back in Plymouth Town.

The two set out to walk along the strand. They spoke of little, however, for still Jack seemed pensive and withdrawn, as though he strove to screw his courage to the sticking point. On her side, Madame was patient, ready to Roger in any way Jack might desire, yet privily diverted by his untoward Shyness.

All of a sudden, Jack seized her by the shoulders and turned her to face him. Derek! cried he, eyes gleaming in triumph, Derek my lad! Thou wilst never guess, in a thousand years, who I be Rogering!

From *Poor Richard's Almanac of Modern Wisdom*

People who live in glass houses shouldn't throw orgies.

The Tale of Jemima Puddle-Fuck

AFTER BEATRICE POTTER

We learn from this delightful little tale that one response to neo-Victorianism is neo-Bohemianism.

What a funny sight it is to see a duck hanging around a flock of chickens looking for a cock!

Listen to the story of Jemima Puddle-Fuck, who was annoyed because the farmer's wife would not buy her a nice big drake.

Her sister-in-law Rebecca Puddle-Fuck was perfectly willing to leave the business of drakes to someone else. "Who wants all those eggs? You have to sit on them for twenty-eight days, Jemima. You know you wouldn't. You have ants in your pants. You couldn't do it for even one day, before you wanted to start partying again."

"Who cares about the eggs? I want a drake!" quacked Jemima.

Jemima became quite desperate. She determined she would look for a drake away from the farm.

She set off one fine spring afternoon along the cart

road that leads over the hill. She was wearing a shawl and a poke bonnet—and nothing else!

When she reached the top of the hill, she saw a lake in the distance. She thought that looked like a good place to find a drake. But it was quite a way away. She would have to fly.

Jemima Puddle-Fuck was not much in the habit of flying. Not actual flying, anyway, though she was partial now and then to a little catnip. She ran downhill a few yards, flapping her wings, then jumped up into the air.

She flew beautifully when she had got a good start. She skimmed along over the treetops with her shawl flying out behind her. Needless to say, her behind itself was all too evident.

Jemima alighted rather heavily near the lake and began to waddle about looking for a convenient humping-place to take her drake when she had found him. She rather fancied a tree stump amongst some tall foxgloves. But seated upon the stump, she was startled to see, was an elegantly dressed gentleman reading a newspaper.

He had black prick ears, sandy-colored whiskers, and a bushy tail on which he was sitting to protect his breeches. "Quuck?" said Jemima Puddle-Fuck, with her head and bonnet on one side. "Fack? I mean, Quack?"

The gentleman lowered his newspaper and looked curiously at Jemima. "I beg your pardon, madam?"

Jemima, who had secretly hoped that he was some kind of drake, was taken aback. Being rather a simpleton, she didn't realize he was a fox and that for him she was a delicacy. She thought him mighty civil and handsome. She explained about the drake and that she was trying to find a convenient humping-place to take him.

"Ah! Is that so? Well, I was fortunate enough to see you while you were airborne," said the gentleman with the black prick ears and sandy whiskers politely. "That drake will be a very lucky fellow."

This made Jemima feel quite curious inside—in the nicest possible way, of course. For the moment, however, she said nothing.

"As to a humping-place, there is no difficulty," continued the elegant gentleman. "I have a sackful of feathers in my woodshed. There, madam, you will be in nobody's way. You may use it in any manner you please." He led the way to a dismal-looking house among the foxgloves. It was built of fagots and turf and had two broken buckets for a chimney.

The gentleman opened the door and showed Jemima in. To afford her the opportunity of examining the humping-place, he then retired, closing the door. The room inside was almost full of feathers—it was quite suffocating; however, it was comfortable and very soft. Jemima was rather surprised to find such a vast quantity of feathers. But they had a most familiar smell to them, which made Jemima feel even more curious inside. It was as if she were surrounded by drakes. Jemima snuggled down into the feathers and imagined she was being cuddled by a nice, big drake. Heavens, how curious she felt now!

Just then the door reopened. The sandy-whiskered gentleman stood there, and lo and behold! he had removed his trousers. Perfectly matching his black prick ears in size and shape, though somewhat lower down, was what seemed to be a third black prick ear.

The sandy-whiskered gentleman snuggled down beside Jemima and, without further ado, took steps to relieve her curious feeling.

"Oh!" said Jemima. "But, sir, you are not a drake."

"Would you prefer me to stop?" said the gentleman.

"Heavens, no!" quacked Jemima. So they played ducks and drakes together for quite some time.

Later that afternoon, they took a stroll together. Jemima waddled even more than usual. She remarked that she vastly preferred the gentleman to any of the drakes she had met.

"That's just as well," he replied, "for there are precious few drakes left in these parts."

Jemima was also concerned about the eggs she would soon be laying. She wanted to go back to the farm and fetch a bag of corn so that once the eggs were laid she could sit on them without leaving.

Eggs, said the gentleman, were unlikely.

But Jemima was certain that before nightfall there would be eggs.

"Very well, madam," said the gentleman. "But I beg you not to trouble yourself with a bag of corn. Why not instead have supper with me? For I would very much like to eat you."

Jemima blushed deep red under her feathers. And she began to feel curious all over again. So she accepted the kind invitation.

"Might I ask you to bring up some herbs from the farm garden to make a savory omelette? Sage and thyme and two onions. For before I eat you, I intend to stuff you."

"Oh, sir!" quacked Jemima, blushing an even deeper shade of red. "Whatever will you say next?"

Jemima Puddle-Fuck was a simpleton. But off she popped to the farm garden to get the herbs people use to stuff roast duck. As she waddled into the kitchen to get two onions as well, she met Kep the collie dog. "What are you doing with those onions, Jemima? Where have you been all afternoon?"

Jemima was rather in awe of Kep, so she told him everything that had happened. He grinned when she described the gentleman with sandy whiskers. He especially liked the part where he had removed his trousers.

Kep asked several questions about the lake and the exact position of the gentleman's house. Then he went off to find some fox terrier friends of his.

Jemima Puddle-Fuck flew back to the lake. She was quite burdened with the bunches of herbs and the two onions. The sandy-whiskered gentleman was sitting once again on the tree stump, reading his newspaper.

"Go into the house, madam," he said—a little sharply, she thought. "Make yourself comfortable, and I will be in, in just a little while, to stuff you and eat you."

Jemima began blushing under her feathers all over again. But she began to feel delightfully curious inside again. She went into the room and snuggled down in the white feathers. Just then she heard a pattering of feet. Someone with a black nose sniffed at the door, then locked it.

Jemima became much alarmed and, truth to tell, a little concerned that she might not get stuffed and eaten.

A moment later there were the most awful growls and howls and squealing and groans. And nothing more was ever seen of the sandy-whiskered gentleman with the black prick ears.

Presently, Kep opened the door. He looked very pleased with himself. There were two fox terriers with him. One of them had a bite on his ear. They looked very pleased with themselves as well.

The three dogs came inside and snuggled down in the feathers.

"Now, Jemima," said Kep. "What about a little something for saving your life?"

"Oh!" quacked Jemima. "Oh, heavens!"

And that's how Jemima Puddle-Fuck came to be stuffed and eaten—in the nicest possible way, of course.

Jeeves and the Problem with Pongo

AFTER P. G. WODEHOUSE

"Jeeves," I moaned, "douse the lights and leave me here to die."

"The light, sir," answered the honest fellow, "emanates not from an electronic source but from the sun. It is two o'clock in the afternoon, sir."

I gripped the pounding bean, as through some mist my recent past began to take shape. Around the hour when birds start hauling breakfast out of the lawn, I had tottered home from P.J. Grady's Bar and Grill down on Broadway, after an evening of lively debate with the free and the brave. While the assembled company had been unable, in the end, to decide whether whales were mammals or fish, the flow of reason had a marked drying effect on the tonsils, and several gallons of P.J.'s finest had passed over same, heading south. Hence the pounding b. Also the unseen hand with the drill.

"Of your restorative," I croaked, "bring me not a little."

"It is in readiness, sir," quoth he, and proffered the mirror.

Not so long ago, Jeeves's usual solution to the young master's excesses was a fierce brown fluid, concocted of ingredients known only to him, which one tossed off with a single manly gulp. Ever since we moved to New York though—due to some rather unsporting new tax laws they've bunged on the books back home—the blighter has managed to reduce this hell-brew to a fine white powder, which you introduce, via a straw, into the beak.

Anyway, the stuff did the trick. The heart jumped like a kangaroo on a pogo stick, the eyes made several complete revolutions of the sun, and for a while someone walked around inside the nostrils, sandblasting them. Shortly thereafter, a sweet numbness crept across the old map, birds began to tweet, and life seemed once again to hold some meaning.

"We wish breakfast, sir?"

As a rule the fragrant eggs and b. are *de rigueur* at this juncture, but for some reason the cheery red McDonald's packet did not beckon.

"No," I caroled, "let's go on to the main event. What's in the post?"

"A disconnection notice from the NYNEX Telephone Company, sir, a rather gloomy report from our stockbroker, and a telegram."

"A telegram, i'faith! I thought they'd gone the way of spats and toppers."

"Amongst a certain class of people, sir, spats, top hats, and telegrams are still regarded as correct."

And he handed me the missive. It read: "Raven nork money. Sensual meat forty prepper written wimpy beast agadir."

It has always run in the Wooster family to be something of a whiz at tongues, and Bertram is no exception, provided the dialogue doesn't go too far beyond "How about a spot of lunch?" But I must admit this left me at the starting post.

"What species of drivel have we here, Jeeves? Is it code?"

"I fancy, sir, that the message was transmitted by someone for whom English is not a first language. I believe the message reads: 'Arriving New York Monday. Essential we meet for tea. Prepare to return with me. Best, Agatha.' "

I reeled. This Agatha, prenom. Aunt, is an avenging relative of the first order. Class AA Jumbo Wart would not be too strong a term. Having fixed me in the family album as its premier chump, she has decided that her mission in life is the improvement of my mind. A decided bird of ill-omen, whose appearance always means Fate is sidling around to one's rear with a sizable section of lead pipe.

"But, Jeeves, this is frightful. Monday is already upon us."

"Indeed it is, sir."

"If the aged pill is winging it all the way over here, she must have a killer bee in her bonnet."

"Given Mrs. Spenser Gregson's reduced circumstances, sir, the trip cannot have been lightly undertaken."

The future looked scaly. But the stiff upper lip of the Woosters has been tried in the furnace before. I adjusted the monocle as Seigneur de Woustier adjusted his before Agincourt.

"Lay out the raiment fair, Jeeves," I said in a level voice. "To show that I care not a fig for the coming ordeal, I intend to take a spin in the park."

Winter suddenly blew across the sunny chamber. Icicles formed on the monocle.

"Am I to understand, sir, that you wish me to prepare the sporting equipment?"

"Yes, Jeeves," I said quietly, bending the man to my will, "and eftsoons if not sooner."

A certain reserve had crept into the happy household of late, touching upon an acquisition I had made, which, to my mind, placed me squarely in the ranks of the snappy dressers. Jeeves has always been a trifle sticky in matters sartorial, and these reactionary hackles of his had shot up like frightened grouse upon my adding to the Wooster wardrobe a pair of absolutely corking Rollerblades. They were the kind with big plastic wheels, bright enough to power a small African nation, harmoniously united with bright red plastic boots. Jeeves took an instant dislike to the new arrivals.

"Impermissible with all types of wear" was his verdict, and that was that. I admit I could see his point in the matter of dressing for dinner. Definitely out, black tie and roller-skates. But when it came to the off-duty ensemble, to the carefree bachelor's daily biff through the park for example, I mean hang it all, this is the twentieth century.

What was needed, of course, was the mailed fist. Force, as some Russian once remarked—Ivan the Great, I think it was, or Peter the Terrible—has its role in history. This time, as before, it worked. The old mailed f., I mean. Utterly crushed, the bloke went about his appointed tasks, handling the young master's wheels with the respect they deserved and not, as is his wont, like a pair of overripe halibut. Then he grabbed the trusty lid and announced that he was off to resolve our misunderstanding with the phone company.

I am generous in victory and, in deference to his feelings, waited for him to tootle off, before actually donning the transportation. This is a ticklish business, which even for the seasoned professional can hardly be considered a breeze. It was not until a tense half-hour had passed that I was all skated up and ready to blade.

At which point the front doorbell rang.

Well, you say, so jolly what? Pop along and answer it. But it wasn't that easy. Once your toes and heels and whatever else goes to make up the average set of trotters are replaced by eight independently-minded wheels, life becomes a tricky prop. Wheels lack decisiveness. While one lot edge toward the front door, the others feel that *la chambre de monsieur,* due south, is a better bet. So it was on this fateful day. Meanwhile, the doorbell continued to ring like the dickens. Quick thinking was vital. In a flash I had dropped to all fours and was beetling toward the noise.

As you no doubt realize from subtle hints I've dropped about the place, the scene of operations has lately shifted from London to New York. Now, New York isn't London. Not that I have beef one about Manhattan. The metrop. still fizzes from dawn to dusk and vice versa. But there are certain things a fellow can do in London that a fellow can't do in New York, if a fellow wants to continue his studies at what my friend Murray down at P.J.'s refers to as "the school of life."

Take front doors. In London, while it's not considered brainy to leave one's portal ajar and the message "DO DROP IN" hanging from the lintel, one can at least respond to a visitor's summons with a cheery 'Ullo-'ullo-'ullo. Whereas in New York, one is better advised to poke a machine gun through the letter box, fire a few bursts, and then ask questions. This I forgot. So chuffed was I at actually making it as far as the bally front door that, heedless of danger, I flung it wide. The 'Ullo-'ullo-'ullo froze on my lips.

For there stood without a most unappetizing cove. A shortish, nastyish, you might almost say brutishish, cove. One of those coves whose election, even to a club such as my own, the Drones, would not be a foregone conclusion. A cove who seemed intent on doing some violence to you, or to his mother or to a passing infant, that would result in his (the cove's) financial gain.

The cove launched into a foreign tongue, which, with its unhealthy emphasis on vowels, I took to be from some sunnier clime. The word *"dinero"* made several noisy appearances, also a term I had occasionally heard addressed to Jeeves in the local bazaar. This word, if word it was, sounded as though the utterer had cleared his throat preparatory to spitting, changed his mind, and come out instead with something in the general area of "heaves." Our conversation, thusly, went rather like this:

COVE: *Dinero* (large amount of foreign tongue), heaves *dinero* (foreign tongue) heaves!
Cove hauls self to feet and by dint of severe shoving about sternum propels same backward into living room.
SELF: Gosh, I say, dash it, look here, don't you know . . . ?!
COVE: (f.t., f.t., f.t., ad lib.) *dinero,* heaves, *DINERO!*

Dialogue ends as self fetches up against small table, destroying several owl figurines. Cove produces gun size of hunting boot.

Points it at self.

What happened next is not clear. As you can see, up to this point, I had pretty much held my own, but the cove's fowling piece definitely gave him the edge. Legging it seemed the better part of valor.

"Sorry, laddie," I chirped, "important luncheon engagement. Must look slippy."

And I aimed myself at the door. The cove, though, had other ideas. So did the wheels. Developing wanderlust anew, they departed for various points of the compass. The cove grabbed me. I grabbed the cove. We rumba-ed back and forth across the rug for a while, and then the world became a sort of macedoine of wheels, burst cushions, broken furniture, and cove-trousering. There followed an explosion somewhat like the entire city of New York falling off a cliff, everything went black, and I presumed that, the full and active having drawn to a close, Bertram was now dearly departed. It was not to be. While I, if you see what I'm driving at, was. As the mists cleared, I discovered that I was reclining, not on a cloud, but on the cove. He was spread-eagled beneath me, the artillery several inches from his right hand, and something from his northernmost regions was rather mucking up the Axminster. I dismounted, covered the cove with the pistol just in case, and shook the lemon to expel various small fowl that had taken up residence.

"Is anything the matter, sir?"

Even from the kneeling posish, I leapt a good foot. It's uncanny, but Jeeves has this knack of just appearing in places. He seems to be able to sort of radio himself from one spot to another. You think he's miles away, then suddenly he's at your elbow, brimming with respectful zeal.

"Jeeves, I say, what the deuce is all this?"

"You appear to have shot the gentleman, sir."

"I do?"

"Yes, sir."

"Ah."

Short pause. Jeeves hovered politely.

"Dead, would you say, Jeeves?"

"The gentleman has all the marks of being deceased, sir."

"And I did it?"

"The essence of criminal law, sir, is that one is innocent until proven guilty. However, you are holding a potential murder weapon, sir, which doubtless bears your fingerprints, and you are kneeling beside a dead person."

"You're sure about the dead bit?"

"Quite, sir."

"These are deep waters, Jeeves."

"Yes, sir."

"Perhaps we could wipe off the old howitzer, stick it in his mitt, and say it's suicide."

"An ingenious plan, sir. However, the question might arise why the gentleman chose our flat to end his life."

"Jeeves, I do wish you'd veer away from this dead-person, end-of-life stuff. It's morbid."

"Of course, sir. I am most sorry, sir."

"You are right to this extent, Jeeves. We have been lumbered with a stiff."

"Yes, sir."

"So the question is, and here I want you to follow me closely for it is the very nub—what do we do with the remains?"

"I regret to say, sir, that nothing immediately suggests itself."

Just like that. Minus something centigrade. The blighter might just as well have been a cod or robot. No hint did he give of clustering round the young m. in his hour of darkness. Then I saw all. It was incredible. In the midst of Armageddon, the man was still miffed about the Rollerblades! The iron entered my soul by the bucketful. Very well, then, said the inner Wooster, alone. I drew myself up to my full height—which I must confess was a trifle rough on the kneecaps—and fixed the man with a diamond-hard gaze.

"Oh?" I said, and I meant it to cut deep.

"Sir?"

"Nothing, you regret to say?"

"I fear not, sir."

And he withdrew.

Frankly, left on my tod, I experienced a certain flatness, as though some superior force were letting the air out of my tires. To dispose of cove, one, shortish, deadish, was not exactly the work of minutes. I could bung him in the cupboard, but my knowledge of similar items, e.g., hung pheasants or Things in the Road, suggested that this would soon become a pretty niffy proposition. The simple shove-out-the-window would be a bit unfair to passing citizens, who, whatever their shortcomings, hardly deserved to be beaned by falling coves. And over it all hung the dreadful spectre of Aunt Agatha, even now winging her way Bertramward. To sum up, it appeared that throughout a long and distinguished career of landing in the soup, I had rarely found the bisque quite so far above the wellingtons.

And then it came to me.

I laughed a careless laugh and rang for Jeeves. So the fellow thought he had me bested! We would see. As he streamed through the door, I placed my fingertips together and glanced at him from beneath lazy lids.

"Ah, Jeeves!"

"You rang, sir?"

"Jeeves, I have formulated a plan. A modest plan to remove the aforementioned remains. Bend the ear. Herewith the wheeze. You will clean up the residue to a respectable degree and place on his head some suitable species of large hat. Sunglasses would also be in order. Then, feigning slight tipsiness, I will escort the remains—let us dub them Pongo—to the street, as if he and I were in a blotto, oiled, or sozzled state. There I will hail a passing hansom, insert Pongo in it, give the cove's destination as a far distant place, pay the fare in advance, and melt away like a thief in the night."

"If I may be so bold, sir, there are alternatives—"

"Thank you, Jeeves. That will be all."

I rose, and as if Fortune herself smiled upon my plan, actually managed to Rollerblade out the door.

It is a mark of Jeeves's sterling qualities that once he realizes I intend to take a firm grasp on things, he buckles to and assumes the role of a cog in the well-oiled plan. By the time I'd shed the blades, he had the remains cleaned up, be-sunglassed, and propped against the hatstand, ready for departure. He had even procured a couple of those odd plastic caps New Yorkers sport these days—the kind that have things written on them, and are supposed to make you look like a paid-up member of the many-headed. He then draped the late one convincingly about my person and bid me farewell with that icy British calm Mrs. Drake no doubt displayed as her hubby biffed off to bonk the Armada. It was in the lift that I began to get some inkling of just how ticklish this operation might be. Supporting the cove was no problem, although he felt, and indeed smelt, rather like a sack of onions. No, the problem, as ever, was people.

The Wooster tents are presently pitched in a smallish apartment house described by Jeeves as being "just off Central Park West," which, if you're given to a fairly elastic interpretation of the words "just" and "off," it is. Solid citizens though the inmates of this joint may be, the neighborhood is not what you'd call top-notch, so they see somewhat more than their share of those ups and downs that give life in the old metrop its special zip. It was with no small concern, therefore, that I observed the reactions of these hard-boiled eggs as they entered the lift. They huddled in the corner farthest from us. They whispered feverishly amongst themselves. They jumped like performing fleas every time the cove's head flopped back and forth. All in all, the two-drunks-stagger-ing-home routine seemed to attract rather more atten-tion than I would have expected in a city packed with drunks staggering home.

The lobby, however, was deserted and picking my way through a rich mulch of wrappers, broken glass, used car-parts, and the occasional child, I staggered without.

Take it from me—if you intend to get drunk in New York with a pal and then put in a spot of staggering, don't expect to rent space in the average hackney. Official pol-icy when it comes to two staggering drunks is give the widest berth poss. If necessary, drivers may even mount the opposite sidewalk. Also advised—the foot on the gas. The steady stream of bilious vehicles bouncing down Co-lumbus Avenue hewed very close to the official line. A couple slowed down to sniff round my ankles, as it were, but took off as soon as Pongo began to flop. In conse-quence, after what seemed like several hours of alternate flipper-waving and Pongo-hitching, I began to feel that my plan might need a little refinement. The brow was distinctly bedewed and a small crowd had begun to gather.

And then, of course, there was the kid.

As a rule, I am not a kid-despiser. They can be jolly additions to the assembled company, provided they stick fairly closely to the old seen-and-not-heard stuff. New York kids, however, do not follow this simple guideline. Modern thought has had its frightful way with them. If a New York kid wishes to have words with you, he dis-penses with the formal introduction and gets right down to it. If he wishes to blow a large plastic bubble in your eye, he does so without let or hindrance and often em-phasizes his point by leaving a lot of it on your lapel. If he wishes to mimic your face or your voice—and some of us have more mimicable faces and voices than others—away he mimics. In short the world is his oyster. This kid was no exception.

"Hey, mister, are you junkies?"

"Am I junkies? What?"

"You hooked on drugs, mister?"

"No no no no no. We're drunk. Smashed. Stewed to the gills. Absolutely potted. Toddle along now."

"You're not drunk. You're stoned on drugs. You crave drugs, right?"

"No thank you. Not today."

"Your friend looks dead. Has he OD'ed on drugs?"

"You don't seem to cotton, laddie. He's not dead. He's drunk. Dead drunk, what? Ha, ha!"

"No he's not. He's dead. Is he going stiff yet? Can I feel him?"

"I say, look here . . ."

"Are you a pusher?"

"How about some nice sweets?"

"My mom thinks you're scum. She thinks scum like you oughtta be shot down like dogs. What are sweets?"

"Candy. Candy bars. Jolly nice, candy bars. If you go away, I'll buy you some."

"How can you buy me some if I go away?"

The old persp. now resembled a monsoon. Pongo insisted on strict adherence to the laws of gravity. Then the kid's mother made her entrance.

"Maurice, get away from those men! You'll catch their diseases."

She was a bimbo of considerable avoirdupois, this mother, with hair like a small nuclear event. She approached me as if I were a cross between a grizzly and a leper, and grabbed the offspring.

"Hi, Mom. They're junkies. He's a pusher. His friend's dead. He OD'ed on drugs. He's going to buy me some candy."

You know the expression "her face darkened"? This is inaccurate and sloppy wordmanship. Actually the face turns the color of rare sirloin steak. The inside bit. Puce I'd call it.

"Candy?! You filthy scum!"

"Madam, I was merely trying to—"

"Scum like you oughtta be shot down like dogs!"

"—pop along. Toodle-oo!"

"Oh, no, you don't, you scum. I'm calling the cops!"

At these dire words, even the impregnable Wooster facade twitched a little. The bouillon, which had been bubbling merrily about my midriff for the past few hours, now closed over my head. Here was I, all agog to put the max. distance poss. between self, dead cove, and the constabulary, whereas Mama Bimbo wished to make of us one big happy family. What I needed most at this juncture was a good stiff brandy-and-s., and a couple of hours of calm reflection. It was not to be. Events now began to unfold at dizzying speed.

It's a curious thing about the gendarmerie, but wherever I've traveled, I find they have an uncanny knack of being extremely absent when you need them most and extremely present when you don't. Now, as ever, they ran by the book. Around the corner came a battered patrol car, hanging out of which, like some hideous growth, was one of the nastier specimens of New York's Finest.

"Stop!" commanded she of the mushroom-cloud hair. "This gentleman needs help!"

"Yeah?" said the specimen, turning a fishy eye on Pongo and myself. "Which one?"

In the circs., this had a certain uncalled-for flavor,

and I was about to register a formal complaint when La Bimbo served me a scorcher.

"Tell him what's wrong with your friend, scum."

The Finest and she gazed at me like two dogs waiting for a biscuit. Or two biscuits. Or, more accurately, like two dogs who, if they do not get two biscuits, will take the equivalent out of your leg. I opened the mouth and gurgled.

The law growled something to something inside the car and began to spoon himself out of his seat.

Friends of Bertram, loyal to a man though they be, will nonetheless admit, if pressed, that he is not in the front rank of fast talkers. And this is just. The glib explanation does not, it is true, spring fully formed from my lips. There is a tendency for the Wooster jaw to hang slack and for a noise to emerge not unlike the last of the bath water going down the drain. But when it comes to action, none is my equal. My reflexes are as lightning. And should I be confronted by the forces of l. and o. while burdened with a rapidly stiffening cove, I know exactly what to do. I grab the carcass by both ends and leg it up the nearest street.

Pretty nifty, you say, and you're absolutely right. But there was one drawback. Instead of boldly pursuing me, with truncheons erect and stern cries of "Hoy, you, stop in the name of the law!"—these blighters unleashed in my general direction several thousand bullets. A bit thick, really, when you consider what I'd already been through, but there it was. Bullets had entered the picture and seemed likely, in due course, to do the same to me.

By chance the street I'd chosen was only one away from my own. A number of empty lots grace this thoroughfare and one of them gives upon the rear of the Wooster residence. Traversing it, you arrive at a base-

ment door, leading in turn to a laundry room, and thence
to the sanctuary of the lift. It was the work of seconds to
maneuver Pongo through the door, round the washing
machines, and into the lift. Mercifully no one got on, and
in a jiffy I was approaching the familiar threshold.

I must say this for Jeeves. He does not crow. He does
not cackle and point the finger and shriek "I told you
so!" He just opens the door with a sympathetic expression, helps you dump the stiff on the mat, and listens
politely while you fill him in on recent events.

"I had anticipated some such difficulty, sir, in aban-
doning the corpse."

"You were right, Jeeves. The one thing the av. New
Yorker does not seem to need is, as you put it, a corpse.
What about the gendarmes, though? They're hot on my
trail."

"Buildings of this type, sir, are not ones the police
enter lightly. You have little to fear from that quarter."

"You make it sound as though there's some other
quarter."

"Yes, sir. In your absence, Mrs. Spenser Gregson
called from the airport. Her arrival is imminent."

Aunt Agatha! In the excitement of trying to unload
Pongo, I had completely forgotten about the old bat. For
a sec. the onion floundered about like a crab in boiling
water. Then my icy calm returned.

"Well, we'd best bung Pongo in a cupboard."

I grabbed old P. by the dogs, but the fellow made no
move to help.

"What is it, now, Jeeves?"

"I fear, sir, that in Mr.—er—Pongo's advanced state
of rigor mortis, it will be impossible to insert him in a
cupboard."

At which point the doorbell rang. I easily equaled the world high-jump record.

"Aunt Agatha!" I hissed, if one can hiss "Aunt Agatha!" "We're done for!"

"Possibly not, sir. If you would oblige, sir—?"

He grabbed Pongo. Together we lugged him into the living room, where Jeeves sat him in a chair by pinning his feet to the ground with a small but chunky coffee table. He adjusted the hat and the dark glasses and shimmered out.

What he had in mind was beyond me, but there was no time for inquiries. I heard the ringing tones of flesh and blood without, and after some exchange, Jeeves poured the old pestilence through the door.

"Mrs. Spenser Gregson, sir."

"You may bring in the tea, my man. Do not serve those so-called English muffins. They are quite inedible."

"Yes, madam."

And dash it, if he didn't disappear, leaving me at bay, with aunt, corpse, and not the foggiest what to do. I tried to block her view of Pongo as she dropped anchor. I was shaking like a leaf.

"Hello, Aunt Agatha."

"Bertram, you look positively dreadful. Just because you reside in America is no excuse to let yourself go to pieces."

"Absolutely not, Aunt Agatha. Quite right. Trifle warm out, of course."

"Don't talk nonsense, Bertram. The weather is distinctly chilly. And stop shuffling around the room in that absurd manner. Sit down."

As you've no doubt gathered, extended debate is not one of Aunt Agatha's strong points. If she tells you to stop shuffling, you stop shuffling. And when I stopped shuffling, she saw Pongo.

"Good gracious, Bertram. I had no idea we had company. Where are your manners? Kindly effect introductions."

If at that moment I had been entered in the New York State Turbot Imitating Championships, I would have swept all categories.

"I—I—I—"

"Come, come, Bertram! This is most embarrassing!"

"Pongo!" I yodeled.

"Pongo?" echoed the aunt.

"Yes, Pongo!" Having spent my all, I pointed at him for added emphasis. The auntly lips came together in that way that makes you wish she'd been strangled at birth.

"Just Pongo, Bertram?" she asked menacingly. "Not Mr. Pongo, at the very least?"

Just then, Jeeves streamed in with the tea trolley.

"Jeeves!" I gasped. "Explain!"

"Of course, sir. Mrs. Spenser Gregson, allow me to introduce Señor Pongo de Vega. Señor de Vega, madam, is an artist of some note in his native country of Colombia. He is a member of the neo-Nihilist school of painting, whose adherents have vowed not to communicate in any way with the world until all forms of graphic art have been liquidated. Mr. Wooster has much interested himself in Señor de Vega's work, madam."

And he withdrew, leaving me, as far as I could see, even further up the creek. The aged relative, having established that Pongo was not a charter member of the Almanach de Gotha, brought the bow round for a broadside.

"Bertram, I must speak to you on a family matter of

the utmost delicacy. Would you communicate to Señor
de Vega that we desire a few moments alone?"

"I—er—"

"Surely even you can accomplish something as simple as that?"

"Well, you see, as Jeeves pointed out—"

"Bertram!"

"Oh, dash it! Listen, Pongo, old thing, could you give
us a couple of secs. for a natter?"

Pongo couldn't, of course, and sat staring at us like a
Buddha with a keen interest in jazz.

"Bertram, this is impossible!" stage-whispered the
flesh and b. "Can you not do something?"

By now a small Niagara Falls was irrigating the nether
garments. Why had Jeeves ditched me in this pickle? Was
he still squiggle-eyed about the Rollerblades? What had
become of the old feudal loyalty? And then Aunt Agatha
took matters into her own hands. Turning to Pongo, she
raised her lorgnette and gave of her best. Even in his condition, Pongo must have felt as though two gimlets were
boring into him. Or worms perhaps.

"Señor de Vega," intoned the Bird of Ill Omen,
"would you do us the honor of leaving the room? It is
imperative that my nephew and I speak—in private!"

I fully expected Pongo to rise meekly and leave the
room. Even dead, I would have. But this corpse was made
of sterner stuff. He didn't budge. And so, raising herself
to her full nine feet eleven and a half inches, the scourge
of my life, Agatha, Aunt of Aunts, approached Pongo and
applied the gimlets to the top of his skull.

"Mr. de Vega!!" she thundered.

And she shook him.

Pongo's reaction was dramatic. His legs, no doubt
disgruntled at being bent out of their natural contour for

so long, burst free. The coffee table fell over as did everything on it. With a sort of silent *boing,* Pongo resumed his L-shape, toppling backward into a bookcase. Aunt Agatha stood gazing down at the debris in horror.

"Bertram," she cried, "this man is dead!"

"Perhaps he's just asleep."

"Bertram! Explain this cadaver!"

"The explanation is simple, madam."

I had been longing for that voice as the hart heated in the chase pants for cooling streams. The next moment I was not so sure.

"Mr. Wooster shot the gentleman, madam."

"What!?"

My sentiments entirely. Given what the young master had been through, this didn't seem to come up to the usual high standards of the legendary fish-fueled brain. For one thing, it was true.

"The deceased person, madam, was in life a 'pusher' or street dealer in illegal substances. He came here seeking redress for an imagined slight, an altercation ensued, and Mr. Wooster summarily dispatched him."

"Bertram, is this true? Think of the Wooster name! The family escutcheon!"

"I—"

"If I may be permitted to speak on Mr. Wooster's behalf, madam—in our reduced circumstances, to which I feel sure you must be sympathetic, Mr. Wooster has had to turn to gainful employment to maintain our standard of living—"

"I'm glad to hear that, but—"

"Our present source of income, madam, is international drug peddling."

"Here, I say, Jeeves—!"

"Drug peddling?!"

"Yes, madam. Mr. Wooster has many persons such as this under his control. The slightest insubordination must be dealt with firmly."

"But this is monstrous! I shall go to the police forthwith!"

"That would be unwise, madam. The police are well aware of Mr. Wooster's activities. They have, as the local argot puts it, 'been taken care of.' "

"In that case, I shall go to the consulate! I shall—"

Jeeves now produced a gun several foot-sizes larger than the cove's. Aunt Agatha gave a little shriek and cowered back against the wall. The cowering was something I'd never seen her do before, and I must say, it warmed the cockles.

"Much though we regret these measures, madam, the nature of our business makes them necessary. You will now leave for the airport and return to London. I need hardly point out that since Mr. Wooster's operation is international in scope, he has agents in every European capital."

You had to admire the aged one's spunk. Even now she didn't give up completely.

"Bertram, I warn you, this is the end! You will be cut off from the Woosters root and limb! I—"

Jeeves loosed off a round at her feet.

"Madam, I do apologize—"

But Aunt Agatha was already halfway down the corridor, squawking like a demented ostrich. Thus she passed from the presence. I turned to Jeeves. The fellow really had gone too far.

"Bit drastic, Jeeves, eh what?"

"Not at all, sir. Mrs. Gregson's purpose in visiting you was to accompany you back to London for a marriage ceremony."

"Well, that's not so awful. Whose marriage?"

"Your own, sir. To a Miss Thistletop-Stynge."

"Good Lord! How do you know that?"

"Mrs. Gregson sent several communications prior to today's, sir, outlining the match in detail. I fear I omitted to bring them to your attention."

"Great Scott!"

"Quite, sir. A most unsuitable young lady. Her father manufactures plastic furniture."

"Egad!"

A shudder passed through my frame. Plastic furniture! I suppose someone has to do it, but I mean to say.

"Close shave, eh, Jeeves?"

"Very, sir."

"Still, I do feel a bit bad about Pongo."

"There's no need for guilt on that account, sir. His demise was long overdue."

"Jeeves! You mean you knew this character?"

His manner grew a trifle distant, I thought.

"We have mutual acquaintances, sir. They will be happy to arrange for his disposal."

I looked from Pongo to Jeeves and back to Pongo. There was the minor matter of the wrecked living room. Otherwise the sky was blue. I fancied I heard a bird chirp. For the first time in one of the longest days of my life, the madrilene seemed barely above shoe leather.

"Jeeves, it looks as though you've done it again."

"There do not immediately appear, sir, to be any loose ends."

Something in the man's voice made me start. I gazed at him keenly. He pocketed the gat and met my eyes with the usual polite deference. Then I twigged. I took the plunge.

"Jeeves—"

"Yes, sir."

"Touching those Rollerblades—"

"Yes, sir?"

"You may do with them as you wish."

"Thank you, sir. I have already taken that liberty. Tony the super is at present in the lobby, practicing what he refers to as 'kneelies.' "

For a moment the vision stabbed at my heart. The orange wheels, the bright boots . . . But we Woosters are not the kind who cling to the dead past.

"Jeeves, you have done well."

"Thank you, sir."

"Despite the advanced hour, this calls for a restorative."

"Very good, sir."

"And I don't mean the liquid sort!"

"Very good, sir."

"What ho, Jeeves!"

"What ho, indeed, sir."

From Crack to Riches: A Screenplay

BY JANET RENO

Janet Reno, the beloved attorney general who some unkind souls hold responsible for one of the worst official massacres in U.S. history, recently berated TV networks for glorifying violence and negative role models. She offered, instead, her own, more edifying teleplay. This is it.

FADE IN:

1. NIGHT. A DIRTY, FILTHY INNER-CITY STREET IN WASHINGTON, D.C.

Sitting on the stoop of an abandoned tenement building or "crack house" is LATISHA HAWKINS, a beautiful twenty-five-year-old African-American female who would have the quiet dignity of a hard-working mother if she weren't hopelessly addicted to crack. With LATISHA is her son JENKINS, a handsome fourteen-year-old African-American teenage male who would be valedictorian of his high school if he weren't running numbers to pay for his mother's habit.

The two of them are being filmed by a "second-unit" camera crew from X-PLOITATION Productions, a huge Hollywood company specializing in television fare packed with gratuitous violence and negative role models for the sake of ratings.

TELEVISION DIRECTOR

Hey, Latisha, let your tongue hang out your mouth. That will present an even more negative image! Yeah—like that! Attagirl! Now pull your shoulder strap down so's I can see some skin, baby! Yeah—like that. Attagirl! Now—

JENKINS

Yo, my man, when's my mamma gonna git paid?

TELEVISION DIRECTOR

We don't need to pay your mamma, boy. We can do whatever we like. We're the media. So long!

The camera crew pack up all their equipment and load it into their luxury air-conditioned van and drive away.

LATISHA

I need some dope, baby. You have the money for a "fix"?

JENKINS

Sure don't, Mamma. I sure wish you didn't have this "jones." Then I could quit running numbers and go to high school to become a brain surgeon like I always dreamt of when I was alone in my bedroom, when I had a bedroom.

LATISHA

Those were the days, weren't they, baby? When we had a place of our own, just you and me.

She starts crying.

JENKINS

Right on, Mamma. But those packing crates was sure cold in winter. P'raps someday we could do better.

He starts crying too, poor kid.

LATISHA *(Wiping her eyes)*

Well—time to go turn a "trick" and pay for a "fix."

She gets up off the stoop, with the gait of a woman older than her twenty-five years, say thirty-five at least. JEN-KINS wipes his eyes and goes with her down the dirty, filthy street. It is still night.

LATISHA *(con.)*

Oh, baby, I wish I didn't have to prostitute my body to feed this mean old addiction!

JENKINS

Want me to run some numbers instead, Mamma?

LATISHA

No, baby. I don't want you corrupted no more. You so smart, and a mind is a terrible thing to waste.

JENKINS

Okay, Mamma. Know something, Mamma? Even though you got a "monkey on your back" your words can still inspire me.

LATISHA

Oh, baby!

JENKINS

Yo, Mamma—tonight when you "score," can I have a "taste"?

LATISHA

Sure, baby, why not? Ruined my life, may as well ruin yours!

She starts to cry again. JENKINS comforts her. They are in the middle of the street. A long black car comes round the corner and runs over LATISHA's leg. She collapses, screaming. JENKINS goes to help her.

CUT TO:

The car pulling up, a driver gets out of the front seat.

CUT BACK TO:

C.U. LATISHA and JENKINS.

JENKINS *(Crying)*

Mamma, you all right?

LATISHA

I think my leg's broke. That's good. I'll sue. This will keep me in crack for the rest of my life!

DRIVER

Lady, I'm sorry. I had the light.

LATISHA

Tell it to the judge, baby! I'm suing yo' ass!

CUT TO:

The car. The back door opens and a woman gets out. She is a Caucasian female, about forty, tall, handsome, imposing, authoritative, blonde, and beautifully turned out. This is JANET REYNAULT. She walks over to the scene.

JANET

What seems to be the problem, Gordon?

DRIVER

I ran this lady down, so now she's suing us!

CUT TO:

C.U. JANET, astonished. DRAMATIC MUSIC UNDER.

JANET *(To herself)*

A born attorney!

CUT TO:

2. INT. HOSPITAL ROOM. DAY.

A hospital bed. LATISHA is sitting up in bed with her leg in a lift. JENKINS is at her bedside, holding her hand. JANET stands at the foot of the bed, tall, handsome, authoritative, and imposing. She is wearing a different beautifully tailored outfit. Two nurses tend LATISHA.

LATISHA

Oh, Ms. Reynault, we can't thank you enough! I'm so ashamed that I threatened you. It was the crack talking!

JANET

Don't you worry about that, Latisha. Just get well. Then I'm putting you through law school!

LATISHA starts to cry.

LATISHA

I can't believe it! The streets taught me that miracles like this just don't happen!

JENKINS

And I'm going back to high school to start my medical training. Hey, Mamma, know something else wonderful?

LATISHA

What's that, baby?

JENKINS

Even though you're hopelessly addicted to crack, you're not suffering any symptoms of withdrawal.

LATISHA

Just goes to show, baby, no one needs drugs if they got hope.

JANET

That's right, Latisha. It isn't that leg that's got to heal. You've got to heal yourself!

LATISHA/JENKINS/NURSES

Amen!

CUT TO:

3. INT. APARTMENT. NIGHT.

The poor but tidy home of LATISHA and JENKINS. LATI-SHA sits at the bare wooden kitchen table reading a large legal tome. Ditto JENKINS, except that his is medical.

LATISHA

Wow, the legal opinions of Oliver Wendell Holmes are real eye-openers! I had no idea that the law could be made to work for ordinary people!

JENKINS

You said a mouthful, Mamma! That's some cerebral cortex you got in that head!

They laugh happily. Suddenly there is a banging at the door. JENKINS gets up and goes to the door to listen.

JENKINS

Who's there?

VOICE (*O.S.*)

Yo, Jenkins. It's Papi, yo' mamma's crack dealer. I ain't seen her recently. She need to "score"?

LATISHA

You get outa my building, you human scum. Don't wanna see you no more. I'm clean! Gonna make something of myself. Be an attorney!

VOICE/PAPI (*O.S.*)

An attorney! Ha ha! You ain't nothin' but a crack-head whore, baby. Now open up and "score" some "rock."

JENKINS

Beat it, buddy! You are persona non grata. Haul ass before I kick ass!

CUT TO:

Outside the door. PAPI is turning away with fear in his eyes. Another crack dealer is with him. Fear also stalks his dusky face.

PAPI

Shee, that Jenkins Hawkins sure sounds tough. I ain't messin' with him no mo'!

CUT TO:

4. INT. A HIGH SCHOOL AUDITORIUM. DAY.

Graduation day. The seats are filled with scholars in gowns and mortarboards, and behind them proud parents. JENKINS is addressing them; he is the valedictorian, just as promised in scene one.

JENKINS

So, I say to you, my fellow students: Stay off drugs, don't buy a gun or a knife or a box cutter, turn your backs on violence, dress neatly, wash daily, throw away those rap CDs, boycott negative television, eat well but in moderation, drive defensively, establish good credit early, worship in the church of your choice, and you, too, will be able to skip three grades like me and get into Johns Hopkins!

He waves to his fellow graduates. The auditorium fills with thunderous applause.

MUSIC: "Pomp and Circumstance," very loud and inspiring.

CUT TO:

LATISHA sitting in the auditorium, dressed in a beautiful, stylish Donna Karan suit. She holds a legal attaché case on her elegant knees. There is no doubt that we are looking at a born attorney!

LATISHA can't contain herself. She runs from her seat up the aisle toward her JENKINS, who is being mobbed by his happy classmates. She bursts through the crowd and embraces him as the MUSIC SWELLS.

PULL BACK to include JANET REYNAULT standing in the wings of the stage applauding too, as she beholds the happy conclusion to this tale. She turns to CAMERA. Her fine, keen eyes are just a tad moist. She gives a thumbs-up to us and

FREEZE FRAME

SUPER:

THE END

THEN: OR JUST THE BEGINNING?